STORIES
WE TELL
OURSELVES

SARAH FRANÇOISE is a French-British writer
and translator currently living in Brooklyn, NYC.
This is her first novel.

STORIES

WE TELL

OURSELVES

SARAH FRANÇOISE

An Apollo Book

This is an Apollo book, first published in the UK
by Head of Zeus in 2018

9 7 5 3 1 2 4 6 8

A catalogue record for this book is available from the British Library

ISBN (HB): 9781786697325
ISBN (TPB): 9781786697332
ISBN (E): 9781786697318

Typeset by e-type, Aintree, Liverpool

Printed and bound in Great Britain by
CPI Group (UK) Ltd, Croydon CR0 4YY

Head of Zeus Ltd
First Floor East
5–8 Hardwick Street
London EC1R 4RG

WWW.HEADOFZEUS.COM

To my parents

1. Salt

'THE FAMILY THAT consumes somuchbloodysalt together, stays together,' said Joan, more than once. It was one of the time-honoured love reprimands she serenaded them with at the dinner table.

Her husband Frank sprinkled the stuff liberally on his red meat and hypertension. The children, too, were heavy consumers. Maya, the salt snob, had taken to carrying a precious little tin of Cypriot pyramid crystals around in her purse. At night, Lois ran home from work to float in tubs of unscented Epsom salt, like a drowsy Ophelia trying to dissolve her lumbago. And William's senior-school cloud-tank experimental video project had left concentric white rings on the salt-intolerant screed of the basement.

In the early days of love, the husbands were told of the time Maya had taken up silk-painting, and made her way through bags and bags of ice melt. Lois, said Joan, got a taste for samphire on a school trip to the French island of Noirmoutier in 1988. So taken was she with its rubbery pickled stalks that she turned her bedroom into a salt marsh, and started growing it in Joan's mail-order Tupperware. Joan fed the new husbands her grown daughters' childhood fixations fast and furiously, like tide alerts.

Once, Frank followed the doctor's orders, and cut salt out of his diet completely. When he realised that, without salt, nothing tasted good, he simply readjusted his pleasure/mortality equation. No matter the variables, death was always its own number. 'You'll live longer,' coaxed Joan. Frank saw his long, unsalted life stretch out ahead of him like one of those interminable garden-centre lunches with Joan's father.

The first exception he made was for soft-boiled eggs, which he crowned with just a few flecks of kosher salt. He extended the indulgence to steak. The doctor had also placed a moratorium on steak and, in fact, on all red meat. 'If you keep eating like that, you'll have a heart attack,' said Joan. Frank thought of his heart. His heart without salt.

Joan searched online for what to do in case of a heart attack. 'Have the person sit down, rest, and try to keep calm.' It seemed to her she'd been doing that since the seventies.

'The family that consumes somuchbloodysalt stays the same,' said Joan to her soured husband and to her three pickle babies, who had not been babies since the eighties. One of them – the one with the appetite for salt flakes – even had babies of her own.

She gibed tenderly, reminding them of the boy on the barque, the one who'd forgotten the magic word, the only word that could stop the bewitched salt mill from grinding away. Because of him, the oceans were for ever briny.

'You're practically preserves,' she told them with a snort, ignorant that, in all corners of the family, saline was evaporating and hearts were draining to the beat of new currents.

*

In September 2015, Frank started frequenting an inexpensive restaurant behind the train station called Chez Josée. The restaurant had a white formica bar, a Pacman pinball machine out front, and a small, windowless dining room in the back. It also had Wi-Fi and beef heart on the menu. The beef heart was served braised, with a garnish of green beans or lamb's lettuce.

Frank started frequenting the restaurant not because of the heart, but because of the Wi-Fi, and because they tolerated the dog. The heart came later.

Every Wednesday, he sat at the back of the restaurant and opened his laptop to work on one of two projects: 1) the 'bor' project, or 2) the Caspar David Friedrich project.

The 'bor' project was an exhaustive compilation of French place names derived from the aforementioned pre-Indo-European root. Its purpose was to settle once and for all the toponymic debate surrounding the precise meaning of the syllable 'bor', itself a rare derivation of the root 'bar'. Many etymologists espoused the theory that the inclusion of 'bor' in a place name suggested a protruding geographical formation. There was a certain degree of discord even within this group, and a broad spectrum of interpretation of the word 'protruding', which included everything from escarpments to huts, copses to knolls, via good old-fashioned hills. A smaller number of fantasists on the fringes of the field pretended that 'bor' meant apiary, citadel, etc. – opinions that were refuted in unison by the other camps.

It seemed that 'bor' was all things to all people – the kind of generous imprecision that kept Frank awake at night. And so Frank took it upon himself to resolve the issue once and for all, through exhaustive, map-based research of the Hexagon.

To do this, he combed through the country inch by inch, circling 'bor' hamlets, villages, hills and plateaux on blue French ordnance survey maps. He travelled an average five miles per hour, walking his index finger and tiring his eyes over the blue-green 1:25,000-ratio atlas. Sometimes his eyelid would start to twitch, and Joan was called to squirt artificial tears into Frank's feverish eyes. He organised the place names he stumbled upon in a sophisticated maze of Excel spreadsheets, and highlighted some of his breakthroughs in online cartography forums under the alias Borax.

The Caspar David Friedrich project was a dissertation on the topography of Romanticism that was now twenty years in the making. Forty, if you counted the research. Sixty, if you took into account the conditioning of Frank's childhood. About a year ago, Frank had started publishing instalments of his thesis on a blog, which was followed by a handful of scholars, and almost as many webcam models in the US and Eastern Europe.

Frank saw these projects as his service to humanity – his humble contribution to the keeping of mankind's history. After all, what was geography if not history in relief? Mountains pushed up out of the earth's crust, and then eroded. Their names, too, erupted from language, over time picking up letters and syllables which might later be shed. As for his interest in German Romanticism, it too was born of a seismic vibration.

As a boy growing up in a village of brutalist high-rises just north of Paris, Frank benefited from municipally sponsored summer camps (courtesy of the town's Communist administration), and discovered a love of nature until then untapped. For years he visited the seaside and the Alps, along with other boys and girls whose parents worked on the line in the tyre factory.

Frank loved the ocean but he grew infatuated with the mountains – with their perpetual snow, icy blue steeps, and great solitude. Back home, Frank shared an apartment with his mother, stepfather, brother and sister, and four step-siblings. At summer camp he had his own bunk, carved with the names and obsessions of those who had enjoyed the same high-altitude privacy before him.

From this top bunk he had an exclusive, endless view over the least populous landscape he'd ever encountered. Even when hiking or climbing with his peers and the camp counsellors, Frank felt that his communion with each trail or rock wall was his own private affair.

Years later, as an architecture student at the Beaux-Arts in Paris, he discovered Friedrich, and recognised in the man's paintings a personal, memory-like quality – almost like the recollection of oneself through and by another. *The Wanderer Above the Sea of Fog* was a ten-year-old Frank on his first ascent of the Dents de Lanfon, the Alpine valley below tucked in beneath a blanket of clouds. The young couple on *The Sailing Ship* were Frank and his shipmate Joris – two twelve-year-old working-class boys on a subsidised boat, watching the black sardine sloops skim by in the Baie de Douarnenez.

When he graduated from architecture school, Frank kissed his mother goodbye, packed all his belongings into a red mountaineer's rucksack and bought a one-way ticket to the Alpine town where, forty years later, he now had a weekly date with an animal's plated ticker.

When the starter came out (often an endive and walnut salad), Frank closed the laptop, put it back in its shock-absorbent case and into the leather satchel he'd bought himself last spring while visiting his eldest daughter, Lois, in New York. At home, he slid the satchel into a satchel-shaped shelf on a desk he'd built from breeze blocks and planks. Later, Joan came to think that Frank's matryoshka-ising of his laptop was perhaps the first red flag.

After the salad was gone, Josée herself – a woman with hair the colour of paprika and chenille jumpers in every shade of blue – came out from behind the bar to take Frank's empty plate to the kitchen. She reappeared shortly with his heart (four slices of it), spread out like a fan.

'Votre cœur, Monsieur Frank,' she said, putting the plate down before him. Frank looked at the steaming organ, picked up the salt shaker that was positioned in the centre of the table, where it shared a gondola with the mustard and pepper, and dropped a minuscule tornado of salt onto the meat.

It was in this restaurant that, on 13 October, one month after he got hooked on heart, Frank received a message from his long-lost German girlfriend, Heide.

*

'You're ordering from a prix-fixe menu, and you have the choice between a starter and an entrée, or an entrée and a dessert – which do you choose?' Lois asked Nick on their third date. They were having dinner at an Egyptian restaurant in Queens that Nick had read about online. Lois tried to season her baba ganoush, but the salt had calcified in the tiny, cube-shaped shaker. Above its compacted relic, three brown grains of rice rattled against each other.

'I'd have to see the menu,' said Nick.

'You can't,' said Lois. 'You just have to commit – salt or sugar?'

'I don't know. It depends.'

'It's to see if we're compatible,' she added. 'In a restaurant setting.'

'What would you choose?'

'Starter. Salty,' she said, waving to the waiter. 'Every time.'

'Me too,' said Nick.

Four years later, Nick discovered the made-up French word 'combattable' while peering over Lois's shoulder one day. She was subtitling a documentary about a renowned kora-player from Timbuktu, and had entered the word as a placeholder until she could think of the proper translation. Nick remembered the look of the word, with its two pointed swords in the middle, like a gate between 'combat' and 'table'. He remembered its epiphanic feel, too.

Three years after the word, seven years after the question, he wondered at what point he'd transitioned from compatible to combattable. And it wasn't all passive. Wasn't just something that was being done to him. Nick was aware he'd become unfascinated with Lois. It might even have predated the affair. She seemed to think so.

They'd met almost eight years ago on the 5 a.m. ferry from Fishers Island to New London, Connecticut. Lois was catching a train back to New York after a long weekend at her room-mate's parents' house. Nick had just spent the week dog-sitting for his parents, who owned a house on the private side of the island. There were only three other people on deck that morning. There was no need to share a bench but they did, and later Lois wondered whether it was the exacting intimacy of witnessing the sun rise next to a complete stranger that compelled Nick to break the silence. They found that they had visited the same beaches, on the same days. Attended trivia night at the American Legion on Friday. Sat in the library with their laptops within a day of each other. It was both the first holiday they ever took together, and the last they took apart.

When they got to New London, Nick offered Lois a ride back to the city in his Jeep. His J'Heap, he called it. The car smelled like burning Kevlar, and there was a rusty hole in the floor of the passenger seat that framed the interstate whizzing by.

The rest – as is the rest of any and every thing – was history.

Back then, she was the great coincidence of him – irresistible like any windfall. She moved into his apartment that autumn. Bought him a pillbox in the dollar store to organise the love notes she left for him Monday to Sunday, morn, noon, eve and bed. Painted votives on the bedroom wall to commemorate acts of kindness. One for making dinner and doing all the dishes that Thanksgiving, one for putting up shelves for her poetry books, one for grabbing her with hot summer hands on the Williamsburg bridge in August, and telling her they should get hitched. Turn that graduate student visa into a green card, and keep on keeping each other for themselves.

Lois stole a dish every time they had a meal in a Chinese restaurant. Kept the soaps from cheap weekends upstate and motels on the Jersey Shore. Gathered pine cones when they went camping in state parks. Mementos, she said. You're too good to be true (to me), he said.

This self-preserving intensity lasted about four years.

And then one day, Lois found that Nick could, in fact, resist her – and she him. Over the next three years, the intervals between the remarkable moments of their relationship stretched out, and a mutual resistance infiltrated the landscape of their love. The miscarriage didn't make things easier. It shone a light on their bad bits and poor doings, left the taste of death in their relationship, and a gaping want in the memory book.

They were still one year away from the seven-year itch when she met the Historian at a friend's wedding.

The Historian had written some books about France during the Occupation that Lois later sought out and read. He taught history at Columbia, but preferred to be known as a Historian, rather than a professor of history. His wife didn't fuck him, or fucked him poorly, and needed him, yes, but in a way that was material and cold.

For a while Lois craved only the Historian. The sexiest thing was his pity. He pitied her for her loss – for all the losses. For him, she resurrected traumas from forever ago, like the time she capsized a catamaran in the middle of the lake, and watched the life preserver bob away from her. Or that call at college, from the mother of a boy who'd been found dead in his dorm room. They'd met in a club a few weeks before, and had fooled around on his bed later that night. She left through the window, for added drama, forgetting her bra and socks. The boy's parents had found her number on a Post-it note on the desk and called it. These things from her past, she posited, they explained a lot. 'Hmm,' said the Historian, warming his cold hands on her neck.

The Historian emboldened Lois with his gratitude. He was grateful for her voice, her body and her time – which was never more than the confirmation of his own availability. She made him want, he made her wait. They kept each other busy.

The affair lasted just under a year, although the point at which Lois broke her emotional curfew – the moment at which their communications started to contain the acceptance of the situation they had got themselves into – occurred after four months. According to Nick, the affair lasted ten months. For Lois, it lasted six.

A bit more than a year had passed since Nick found out about the affair, forcing Lois to tell him about the affair. The end of the affair was sudden and violent, like a bout of food poisoning. One day, Nick opened Lois's computer and found the emails. Hundreds of them, tracing her complicity with another, confirming an absence he had long suspected. He hadn't gone in there looking, he said, but then again, he couldn't be sure.

The decision to reignite that great coincidence of theirs after what Lois had gone and done was brutal, perhaps even reckless. For Nick it felt like forgiving a stranger. And for Lois there was no adjustment – no Dear John letter, no parting reassurance to fuel the pilot light in case things with Nick didn't work out. No chance to miss a man who wasn't her husband.

In the weeks that followed the end of the affair, Lois slept on the living-room couch. She fell asleep each night staring up at the brown spots of rust that haloed the painted tin ceiling. She came to know those muzzy circles by heart – the way they faltered with the receding light until they were only shadows, straddling other shadows. During those weeks, she wished she too was a stain. A stain was never welcome, but eventually it was accepted, and then forgotten about.

She did the things you do on a computer to prevent all contact with someone. Maybe the Historian had written to her his despair over her silence, maybe he hadn't. Maybe he guessed they'd been found out, maybe not. Maybe he and his wife were having sex again. Maybe they'd never stopped. Maybe he'd found someone else. Someone less intent.

Nick asked how often (twelve meetings, sex four times) and where (a bench on 11th Avenue, a coffee shop on 9th Avenue, his office, a Chinese restaurant, their apartment, a playground, a dive bar, a church, the stairwell of a Bikram yoga studio in Chelsea, a dollar store, a record store, the dive bar again), but he never asked why. He asked again and again, eliciting more and more detail, until the affair was stripped of any reason and reduced to a series of inconvenient manoeuvres, slots in a calendar, and ill-fated decisions about time and place.

When Nick let her sleep in the same bed as him again she stayed close to the wall, giving him space, and doing her penance at the same time. For two weeks he turned his back on her. And then one night he slept on his back, reached under her neck and pressed her head against him. It was difficult to breathe in this position and it made her scapula sore, but still she stayed there. There were times after that when she caught him looking at her from across the kitchen, like an enemy. He'd say he was a fucking idiot, that he should have kicked her out a long time ago. She'd say, yes, he should have, and begged him not to.

Lois stopped missing the affair in early June. By then it had been over for seven months. Until that point, the city was just a giant grid that held them both. The Historian was likely in one of eight, ten, twelve places. She could take the subway to one of these places and be metres away from him, perhaps, through concrete and windows and tunnels. He might leave a building, turn a corner and see her there, coming down the sidewalk. What then? Would he shout to her from across the street, call out her name like an old friend? If so, she would have to walk on, pretend not to hear.

Nick believed her when she said it was over. But so what. It being over was just more evidence it had existed. There were lemons in the kitchen cupboard that were almost as old as their relationship, Nick thought. Captured in rock salt, they still shone yellow and showed no sign of corruption. Lois had canned them one night, following Joan's recipe. She'd told him the lemons wouldn't be ready for weeks, and for that reason he'd read the operation as an early act of commitment.

Nick opened one of these jars now, and tipped the lemons into a colander. He put them under the tap and let the water wash out the slime that had kept them desirable all these years.

Without the brine the lemons were thin and translucent, and when Nick took them out of the colander he felt how fragile their flesh was, and how a clumsier hand was all it would take to tear them apart.

*

Joan found out about Heide at the start of November.

Frank had been disconnecting by increments for years, but in the last two weeks of October he'd all but vanished. He spent more and more time in his maps and on his blog (or so he said), and started using his phone for email. Frank, who left things lying all around the house, kept the phone buried deep in his pocket at all times. One day he switched the phone to silent, but still it hummed through his cords, sometimes up to twenty times a day.

At night, instead of falling asleep in front of the ten o'clock news, Frank disappeared into his study and closed the door. It didn't take long for Joan to realise that his newfound appreciation of podcasts was just an excuse to keep the door shut. She grew more and more suspicious, and eventually asked Frank if he'd perhaps adopted a new pre-Indo-European prefix.

The day she hacked into his email, and found it to be full of a German woman she vaguely remembered had preceded her, she sat at the kitchen table for several hours, wondering what to do. If she confronted Frank, he would defend himself against actionable infidelity and accuse her of snooping. Somehow, she suspected, this would become about her prying.

Joan decided to give Frank the chance to extricate himself from this correspondence on his own. She would make him paranoid that she knew, and manipulate a dignified outcome for them both. Frank had no idea why Joan was suddenly playing Wagner all the time. 'She hates Wagner,' he wrote to Heide in late November.

In one of his emails to Heide, Frank complained about his saltless diet. He did not go as far as to use the word 'bland', but Joan read it anyway. She started seasoning their food again with some zeal, grinding salt over his salad and vegetables, and pushing squares of salted caramel chocolate with their after-dinner coffee. 'That'll show him,' she thought. 'Maybe she's trying to kill me,' Frank wrote to Heide.

Joan had craved salt with the two girls, but not with William (whom everybody called Wim), disproving centuries of questionable pregnancy counsel. With Wim, she craved a boy. Her instincts proved dependable, but she already knew this from having once filled out a Jungian personality quiz on the last page of a woman's magazine. Like Pericles, President François Mitterand and, some speculated, Barack Obama, she was an ENFJ (Extrovert, iNtuitive, Feeling, Judging) – anxiously altruistic and logical.

When Frank moved his pregnant wife and daughter out of their cramped apartment in the old town and into the rental house in the suburbs, he'd spoken of a temporary situation. Six months at most. Joan had unpacked only a few boxes, thinking they'd be in the new house before it was time to take out the winter clothes.

Over the next four years, Frank finished a great many houses. Just not theirs.

Every now and again, Joan opened a new box; to find old clothes for the new baby, to revive her Roxy Music records. When her mother died, she tore through three boxes labelled KITCHEN just to exhume the julienne slicer from her childhood. She julienned everything for a month. Frank complained that it looked like play food. Eventually, when the last box was unpacked, it was time to move again.

Wim was almost four by the time they moved into what Joan called the New Chapter house. Lois wanted the room in the eaves – the one with the romantic half-moon window and a long hallway to separate you from everyone else. Maya wanted that room, too, but it was given to Lois, the eldest. Maya and Wim had adjoining rooms with a sliding door that could be opened to increase the play space. Within two years the diplomatic opening was walled up, and their Lego collections kept separate.

The new house, which Frank had designed himself, was like a salt dome. New columns swelled up through the foundations, sprinkling white dust on the children's quilts. Walls were built and later knocked down to expand the dome in useless places, such as too close to the neighbour's precious boxwood hedge. One year, Frank mined the basement to excavate an unsanctioned wine cellar, causing a minor landslide in the garden. They were having dinner on the terrace one evening when the lawn suddenly swallowed the ficus. One room in the basement was soundproofed to watch films in, then waterproofed for a wetroom, then filled to the ceiling with firewood.

Frank couldn't leave the house alone. It was never finished, there was always something that could be improved – or, as Joan put it, worsened, to be improved someday when we're dead. Frank picked at the house like a scab, but it was Joan who couldn't heal.

Once, when Frank was working on an extension for a luxury spa in Switzerland, there was no hot water for ten days. He blamed the new-fangled boiler, and shouted at someone over the phone. He asked to speak to that someone's manager, and then yelled at them. Every night, Joan hauled saucepans and kettles of boiling water to the bathroom, and the girls had to bathe together. One evening after the school run, Joan came in to find Frank hunched over one of his maps with a pencil and a magnifying glass. When he asked for the eyedrops, something in her snapped. She marched over to him and swept the open maps and papers off the table with her arm. Crash went Frank's glass of water as it smashed to pieces on the marble floor. The water puddled between them like a moat, and it was hard to tell the broken ice cubes from the shards of glass.

'Do you hate Papa?' asked Maya, who was ten at the time.

'Hate is a strong word,' Joan answered, rinsing soap out of the girls' hair with water from the kettle.

'So is love,' said Lois.

Eventually the children grew into adults, but the house

continued to toddle. Not everything had developed right. There were empty sockets and live wires poking out of dry wall, full of promise. There were holes in the roof that let in the wasps, which built their nests under the black tiles. The gaping chimney flue had been covered with a blue tarpaulin since 1995.

Meanwhile, Frank became known for his cultured renovations of other people's chalets, and had carved out a niche locally as a green social housing expert. His own, permeable home guzzled heating oil and, at one point, even housed a concrete factory. The house and Joan eroded each other mutually over the years, much like Joan and Frank, but everyone knew, especially the kids, that Joan could be depended on to make a palace out of a mole hill.

So when Maya announced that she, her husband Cole and the kids were coming over for Christmas, Joan asked Frank to do something about the deadly holes in the unfinished parts of the house, particularly the ones with protruding rusty metal rods. Frank's answer was to hang CAUTION signs on the landing and in the garden, and behind the open skylight into his bat cave.

'You must be joking,' said Joan, when she saw the signs.

'What?' said Frank.

'They're five and one, Frank. They can't read.'

Frank took down the signs and replaced them with new ones, depicting a cliff face, a falling baby with an upturned mouth and a skull and crossbones. Joan couldn't help but notice that Frank's Sharpie crag, with its curtain of limestone stalacmites, bore a striking resemblance to Friedrich's *Chalk Cliffs on Rügen*.

2. Leaps and Bounds

WHEN MUMBLED IN your sleep, invincible can sound a lot like invisible. And so it was that, on the night of Thursday to Friday, Nick didn't know for sure how he made Lois feel. The next morning he woke up before her and made oatmeal, sweetening it when he knew she liked it salty.

They had eaten out last night, got drunkish, and watched *Brief Encounter* in a slumberous heap. Nick hoped the warmth would turn into sex, but the warmth just turned into sleep, as it often did.

After Nick left for work, Lois scraped the rest of her oatmeal into the compost bin and took a shower. The bathroom was cold from the inexorable two-inch gap between the window and the sill. The plastic hinges on the window had snapped two summers ago, and now it had to be kept at this height to ensure it didn't pop out of its grooves and kill someone down on Guernsey Street. Nick had cordoned off the window with duct tape and stuck a note to it that read: 'Do not attempt to open this window: it is broken, like the healthcare system.' He'd have written 'marriage', thought Lois, had the broken window not preceded the affair.

Lois opened her mouth under the shower head and let it fill up with hot water. The water dribbled out of her mouth and gathered at her feet, catching up to her ankles because of a clogged drain. She looked at her watch. She wondered if the Historian was having a shower, too. If their two run-offs were combining underground at this very moment, and if that was the closest thing to a reunion they would ever know.

In two days, she would take a bath in her parents' house. Her parents' tub was deep, and never had a scum ring. Their bathroom window functioned, and came with a view of the French Alps. The two nearest mountains tumbled down to the lake and made a rocky valance that framed all the other peaks in the distance. She wondered whether the tiles were up around the tub, or if there was still a border of concrete, gouged to hold stones that might be heavy and Italian and would likely never materialise.

As she rubbed the moisturiser into her face and down her neck, and into the back of her hands, and down her legs that got scaly in the winter, she thought of her mother's beauty products, lined up on the windowsill and in soft woven baskets that slid perfectly inside drawers. Joan compensated for Frank's architectural impasses with finishes she plucked from the pages of *Elle Decoration* and *Architectural Digest*. She poured cans of sealant onto crumbling concrete floors, hid ceiling wires inside paper lampshade decoys, and painted the plywood matte white. The downstairs toilet was a library for her collection of magazines about beautiful, safe, finished homes – homes that existed to be enjoyed, not negotiated.

Lois was looking forward to being in the thick of that familiar balance – somewhere between her father's dreams of an impossible reality and Joan's dreamy magazine realism. Soon. Soon she would be home, using her mother's anti-wrinkle cream combined with a periwinkle night cream, reversing time on a nanoscale. At the end of the holiday her mother would send her home with half a pot of face cream and an open tube or two of something with a rare and pricey fragrance, like quince or milkweed. They would last into the spring, along with the illusion that she was the kind of woman who, like Joan, filed away her moisturisers into categories.

Three dollar bills fell onto the mat when Lois opened the front door. Coffee money: one of Nick's romantic deeds. She never knew when to expect coffee money. Nick's perfect grasp of timing was what made his demonstrations so unpredictable. He came home with just-because flowers, and caught her off guard with his needs. 'Write me a mash note today,' he'd text her, 'or I'll go out drinking all night, and piss in the sink.'

She picked up the money and walked out into the eighth consecutive snow day.

*

Lois knew that hawks were not a common sight along the industrial stretch that fuses Greenpoint to Williamsburg. So what was a hawk doing, perched on the tennis court fence at Bedford and North 12th, at 8.20 on a Friday morning? Why would something as consummate as a bird of prey waste its camouflage on the sloppy grey stuff that fell on New York City, poisoned as it was before it even hit the ground?

It was snowing hard, but at least it was snowing vertically. The hawk's talons made black rings around the frosted steel chain link. Snowflakes came to dissolve on its beak. The snow on the Bedford sidewalk was piled so high that when Lois stopped beneath the hawk, it was only six feet away from her face. The sight of icicles on the steel fence made her teeth ring. Inside her coat pocket, her phone shivered with an incoming call.

She knew it was her mother calling because her mother always called in the morning. But today it was too cold for hands to come out of pockets, even with gloves on. Lois ignored the phone, and eventually it went still. A squirrel rappelled down a sycamore to excavate a quarter cream-cheese bagel from a hill of slush, a few feet away from Lois. It occurred to Lois that, unlike the hawk, the squirrel did not look out of place at all.

For the most part, she thought, everyone is in the wrong place at the wrong time. And those who weren't had their own crosses to bear, such as the burden of a life's work, or martyrdom. Take the New York squirrel: only slightly cuter than a rat, but with much greater benefits. Unlike the rat, which is hated with some hysteria, the squirrel can forage for pizza crust and crumbs out in the open, without fear of man (don't care) nor hawk (in the city, as rare as an orchid).

Take her mother: a good girl from Nottingham who'd sought out the kind of Gallic abandon sold to her by the French New Wave, only to find herself raising three children in a town where you couldn't hope for a decent cup of tea. Or maybe that was being in the right place at the right time. Who even knew.

After it was scooped up out of the snow by the combined action of claw and beak, and during the first few seconds of its rude airlifting, the squirrel looked as bewildered as Lois. They shared this, she and the squirrel: the microscopic passage of disbelief in time. It was between them, and them only. Now the squirrel did look out of place, too high in the sky, and too on its way to dead. And yet it hadn't broken any rule of nature or city.

The hawk seemed to have known what it was doing all

along. Like nothing was a coincidence, not even the drama of its chosen backdrop – the billowing chimneys of the Con Ed power plant on the other side of the East River.

By the looks of things, the squirrel was being carried away to a more secluded perch, somewhere in Queens. Lois imagined a nest under the subway tracks, or in the spire of a Catholic church, perhaps in Corona. Or maybe the bird was headed further out, somewhere on Long Island.

When the hawk was out of sight, Lois continued to walk down Bedford. As she turned to meet Berry, the phone started ringing again. She pulled it out of her pocket. The word FAMILLE throbbed across the display.

'Hello, Mum.'

'Hello, poppet,' said Joan. 'Are you in the street?'

'Yes. I'm always in the street when you call.'

'Are you on your way to work?'

'Yes,' answered Lois. 'I'm almost there.'

Lois passed a woman with a baby strapped to her chest. The baby was wearing a lilac snowsuit and looked like it had been pumped full of air. In the past two years, the city seemed to have filled up with other people's babies.

'Well, I won't keep you,' said Joan. 'I was just calling to warn you.'

'Warn me of what?' asked Lois.

'If you sense any tension between me and your father, I mean, extraordinary tension, it's because things are extraordinarily tense.'

Lois wondered how long before the squirrel got eaten. Maybe by the time she got to the office. Surely birds of prey didn't toy with their catch.

'Oh.'

'Look. I may as well tell you – but don't tell your sister. I don't want this to turn into a big family drama.'

Families are to secrets what holes in trees are to squirrels, and nests under water towers are to hawks: a nest and a refuge, a place to drag your feed back to. When the secrets are spoken, you realise they were there all along – so many reasons to drawbridge into one another's business, and to love each other less, and to love each other more.

'Jesus, what is it? Now you're scaring me.'

'Your dad's been having an emotional affair.'

'Oh,' said Lois. Her mother's use of the word 'emotional' both reassured and irritated her.

'He doesn't know I know.'

'Then… How do you know?'

Joan left the question hanging.

'The weird thing is, I'm not sure how much I care,' said Joan. 'I mean, it makes me livid, but not for the reasons you'd think.'

If Frank didn't know Joan knew, then all the extraordinary tension must be coming from Joan. She imagined her mother giving Frank all kinds of passive-aggressive hell. She pictured her father, disengaged, buckling under the weight of secrets that, at the end of the day, were smaller than hers. She'd never told her parents about the Historian, because she'd fallen short on so much already – career, parenthood, and now marriage.

There used to be a joke about a sleepwalking uncle. He'd often wake Lois and the others up at night, the sleepwalking uncle, slamming the front door open and giving loud soliloquies to the mirror. Lois would sometimes get up and spy on him from the staircase. He'd say funny things about there being eighteen AAA batteries in the cupboard, but no mayonnaise. And then there was that one time when he held the Christmas cactus up to his face and asked if those were tears in its eyes, or if it was only the onions.

He'd sleep-drink too, and make himself enormous sandwiches that wobbled too much, and looked like they'd end up splat on the carpet. And sometimes he'd see Lois spying on him, and he'd bellow out something vulgar and it made her laugh, because it was all in his sleep, and she'd run back to her bed and hide under the covers, and pretty soon all would be quiet downstairs. The next morning her aunt would say, 'Oh, that silly uncle, sleepwalking again,' and she'd add mayonnaise to the shopping list.

'What are you going to do about it?' asked Lois.

'I haven't decided yet,' said Joan.

Lois didn't know what to say. If one of them should have an

28

admirer, surely it was Joan. She was the one who made new friends and stayed current with the old ones, who saw their social engagements as a diversion, not a demand. Up until this point, Lois had always thought of herself as being more like her mother, and less like Frank. Her father had just gone and changed that, simply by being himself.

'I just wanted to warn you. If things are tense, you'll know why. But don't worry, everything else about Christmas will be normal.'

'I'm not worried,' said Lois. 'I mean, not about Christmas.'

'Well, I'll let you get to work. Safe travels. Your dad and I can't wait to see you.'

The snow stopped falling vertically and, instead, started whipping at a diagonal. Somewhere in Corona, a squirrel's neck snapped.

*

Dearest Heide,

My essay on Caspar David Friedrich is coming on leaps and bounds. Or should I say, it is staring cautiously and with considerable support from an oak over the abyss of completion. For completion is an abyss, since it is getting to the bottom of things, which leaves you with nowhere else to go. I suppose it could be a wall, but then there would be no view, and what are we doing if not looking out further, trying to convince ourselves that there is something beyond ourselves, beyond our daily problems, beyond

the instruments of our lives, and the boiler that breaks down, and
the shower nozzle that is all stopped up with calcium deposits, and
will need to be soaked in vinegar again? I think that is why I love
the mountains so – all possibility and no persons.

Joan came into the living room with the vacuum cleaner. She
had done the floors earlier, but was now going around with
the special nozzles: the long skinny one that fitted under the
sofa, the bendy one that went inside the anglepoise, and the
one with the plastic whiskers that floated over the books and
kept them cobweb-free.

Frank stood up and tightened the belt of his old threadbare
bathrobe. The robe was a Christmas present from Lois, when
Lois was two. Joan had done this; she'd picked out gifts for
him from each of the children, until they were old enough to
forget to do it themselves. There was a picture of him wearing
the robe that Christmas, holding Lois on his lap. Lois – her
trademark red helmet bob a mess – was tiny in the picture,
and sucking on the straw of a CANDY chocolate-milk box.
Frank had pinned the picture to the wall of his home office,
and whenever he looked at it he tried to avoid himself, because
he didn't care to remember that he would never be that blithe
or young again.

Frank had been pushed out of his real office in the centre
of town by a cumulation of hindering circumstances such as
the breakdown of the photocopy machine, the shutting-off of

the electricity due to unpaid bills, the loss of a parking space due to unpaid charges, and the uncontrollable expansion of the archive, which had grown like Maya's kindergarten pet tea mushroom.

When Frank bought the office he had a partner, a secretary, a draughtsman and two apprentices. For a while there were even office Christmas parties. These were always held at the height of summer, in a family restaurant called La Frite that had a mini-golf course out front. Lois and Maya believed the place to be crazy posh, with its deep baskets of fried whitebait that came with moist towelettes, and lemon sherbet served in real, hollowed-out lemons.

In the end, the secretary lasted the longest, but possibly saw Frank as a slow-sinking ship, and had the foresight to jump. Joan offered that there were surely other secretaries looking for work in town. But Frank saw all the office-related issues as linked, and solving them one by one felt about as vain as swimming in one of those counter-current pools his Swiss clients seemed to like. Lois and Maya continued to clamour for the real lemon sherbet long after the dog-days Christmas parties ceased, long after La Frite was bulldozed over to accommodate a new car park.

Working from home started off as an indulgence, but before long Frank came to dread the twenty-minute commute to his cold, unclean office, which, in any case, ceased to be a viable workspace at sundown. He weaned himself off the office completely, taking over the guest bedroom with his inky razor blades, toppling piles of binders and tubes of blueprints. He built himself a desk, which was supported by breeze blocks and two sections from the trunk of the old cherry tree the neighbours had lobbied to have him chop down, on the wretched charge that it rained cherries onto their property.

He made a plan to organise the archive, get a storage space, and rent out the old office. They would use the extra money to finish off the house. The plans to empty the office started dying before they were even hatched. Started dying when Frank was but a boy and things around him – father figures included – changed fast and often. By the time December came round, he hadn't set foot in the old office for months.

Joan sucked dust up off the table, circling his laptop and his letter to Heide, which lay hidden behind the landing page of his blog – a home for his musings on German Romanticism and French place names. Frank picked up the computer, walked out of the office and went over to the landing.

I told you last week about my client from Dubai. Well, it looks like the project might go ahead. The client wants to fly me over in the new year to meet his associates. They expect me to bring my wife, I think. The associates want to meet her. But – no, what are you making me say? We must never be in an airport together.

The sound of the vacuum cleaner was accumulating in a corner of Frank's brain, like snow around dust particles. Frank remembered he'd promised to bring the decorations down from the attic. He liked the fact that they still had the straw ones he and Joan bought in the Black Forest, on the honeymoon that killed their first VW.

These days, it was the car that killed the marriage. For some reason, Joan objected to the shit he kept in there – more of the office archive, the occasional McDonald's burger wrapper, items that had been en route to the dump since 2007, the sand and dirt of fifteen years of ownership.

At home he tapped his right foot constantly. The foot was frenetic under the table, the desk, in front of the news at night. In the car the foot had dug a madness-trench under the driver's seat which exposed the metal of the chassis. Joan nagged that the car – like the house – was unsafe, but you didn't catch diseases from Alpine dirt or the stale smell of a Big Mac, and dust in carpet was not a leading cause of traffic accidents, argued Frank.

Last night, I dreamed you had curated a show made entirely of paintings of me. In each portrait I was wearing a different outfit. I was upset because, in some of them, I looked a little old and overweight. One outfit was a white T-shirt with the 1992 Albertville Winter Olympics logo on it, and these pyjama pants J keeps threatening to throw out. The other was a soldier's uniform – the old khaki wool ones. The last outfit was one of your dresses. A dress I remember you wearing that time we drove to Amsterdam. I recall it was pink, or the colour they call salmon, and it had a square cut-out neckline. In the dream you also asked me to proof-read your memoir. I said I couldn't see the writing, only blank pages. You said, have you never heard of invisible ink? It's made with lemon juice. It becomes visible with salt. Frank paused. *In the dream you blended into your surroundings. Like Friedrich's Madonna blends into the mountain.*

The dream had touched Frank's vanity, and made him feel older still.

Dearest Heide, on the eve of my entire family showing up, I must confess that I have no enthusiasm for anything but you, Caspar David Friedrich and my dog.

Downstairs the vacuum cleaner went dead, and Frank heard Joan walk from the living room into the kitchen. A minute later the electric kettle started the wheeze that sometimes made Frank think of murder. He couldn't believe Joan pointed out the malfunction of his car, of his arterial pressure, of his method for remembering which pills to take by lining the tablets on the *Flying Dutchman* CD case, when her own tea kettle was such a lousy piece of equipment.

'Did you get those decorations down, yet?' shouted Joan,

even though he could hear perfectly well now the hoover had stopped.

Outside, the mountains were on their way to silhouettes.

Frank saved the draft and closed the laptop. He thought of going to the fridge and eating something, but decided it wasn't worth it. Joan would only make some comment. Why should he feel guilty about eating from his own fridge? In pure investment terms, he had much more of a stake in the fridge than she did. Frank knew how much harm such a thought might do if articulated out loud. It was never formally agreed between them that Frank would make the money and Joan would raise the children. Things just took that course. Joan often wondered what she might have become, if her becoming had been tethered to something other than the kids.

But Frank did feel guilty. Not from writing to another woman, because that correspondence existed in the world of maps and image searches and Wordpress comments – a world *they* kept reminding him wasn't real. He felt guilty because someone was making an effort this Christmas, and it wasn't him. Someone had gone to the trouble of planning meals and doing headcounts for future feasts. Ingredients were spoken for. The fridge was no longer just a fridge, but a system. He knew that, and he found deference for Joan in the idea that, at least, no one expected *him* to be a good mother.

*

There is another house with veins of slate which sits in an always muddy berth. A salty rain falls on it nine months out of the year. The blue roof goes slick and black, and you get wettest coming in or out of the house. The walls of the barn – the one that lost its head to rotten tiles – are more brittle than Joan's shortbread, and more crumbly than her crumble. Each summer they burst into butterflies that land on the dead power lines that are still tacked to the roof.

The house is more time than place; an HQ for rock pool hunting, a starting point for the activity of chasing sunsets, a bunk bed for muckraking or whispering about the boys next door, who turned from little frogs into suntanned surfers with biceps and mobile numbers, an end point for nights in unlit churches on cliffs, co-sponsored by the tourism bureau and the local coffee-roasting plant.

The house is at the other end of France, where the country throws itself at America and falls 4,400 miles short. Frank bought the house in 1990 for no money at all, from a woman who hated it because it reminded her of her ex-husband. It reminded them of nothing they had ever seen before. They had rented holiday homes like it in the area, but those had running water and brown tiles everywhere, and no German graffiti from the last summer squatters.

The house came with its own well, but the water was no good for drinking, and therefore it was dedicated to wishing. The well had no roof, and the splashes of tossed francs got more promising after every rainstorm.

Everything falls into place in that house, even the rain.

Lois is seven, then eight, ten, fifteen with friends, eighteen with a boyfriend. She makes secret treasure maps with hologram stickers, slides snails up against each other to watch them mate, and gets addicted to chicory. Maya is two years behind and prettier. Lois is the one who names the cows and chickens and makes a game out of touching the electric fence. They all get shocked, and pretend it increases their brainpower. Maya is the one who makes friends with the other kids in the hamlet, and threatens to jump out of the bathroom window when she doesn't get her way. Lois keeps vials of putrid flower water in the barn, which she later decants into her mother's empty perfume bottles.

Then comes William, quite a bit later. The favourite no one resents. He learns knitting with the grannies and woodwork with the sleepwalking uncle, who buys him a special box to cut perfect angles with a saw. He calls it a see-saw. He sets the table for lunch and dinner, and lets his sisters dress him up as a reindeer, even when it isn't Christmas.

Frank, architect, does nothing to this house but give it running water. He lets it be. He gives it over to them, like someone gave over the garden to those sickly fuchsia roses. They fill it with driftwood and noise, and white and blue crockery from the Habitat in Lyon. Lois tells Joan it is like one of those magazine houses, only smaller. Joan beams. Unlike the other house, the ambitions for this house have nothing to do with the house itself, and no one resents its imperfections. The cracks in the wall hide the cigarettes Lois shoplifted on a school trip to Prague. The sleepwalking uncle builds a workbench for all the improvements no one will ever seek.

Joan fills the linen cupboard with antique sheets and mono-grammed pillowcases she buys at the flea market. She finds a farm that will sell her butter. She picks up the butter every week – big doorstops of it, wrapped in kitchen parchment and tied with parcel string. The butter smells like grass, and hides great big crystals of salt that go crunch under your teeth, like grit.

It reminds her of Cornwall. Of dangling her legs over a stone wall, and stealing sips of her mother's shandy. Of going to the cinema in someone else's town. Of licking the dried salt off her forearm, long after a swim. Things don't feel so French here, and when you're up to your knees in ocean, it's almost like you've left the country.

They get used to the hornets, which come back year after year, and Lois decides this is where she'll live when she grows up. She'll be a famous poet and marry one of the surfer boys next door, and their children will learn the vanishing Breton language in the Diwan schools, and breed bunnies as pets.

Frank likes it here. He can be here for ten whole days before he starts missing the vertiginous comfort of the mountains. He can drive to the beach and walk south or north, but eventually the beach stops. He likes the fishermen's suppers, with their plates of steamed langoustines and the plastic boats of yellow mayonnaise that taste just like the mayonnaise his great-aunt used to make. He is happy he could give them this house to spend their summers in, and he is happy to join them there as and when he can.

Maya gets married there in 2009. It's Cole she marries, of course. Cole's family come over from England on the ferry. They rent out the gîtes where Frank, Joan and the kids stayed before they had this house. Maya works on the priest for months to book the local church. It's special to them because once, Frank swept the entire church floor with a key in his mouth and was cured of his toothache. The priest softens when he hears of this miracle, and concedes when Maya raises enough money to restore one of the stained-glass windows. After the ceremony they have seafood platters and cider in the garden, and crêpes for the kids. Joan sits back and watches her middle child, who is now married. Maya is already pregnant with Gitsy. She is happy. Joan is happy. And if Joan and Maya are happy, then they are all happy. It is like chemistry.

That is the holiday house, the one that charts the family like nicks and dates in a doorframe. Their only responsibility is to appreciate and share it.

The other house, the one Joan is vacuuming now, is built on the fault line of Frank's ego.

3. Verbascum

RODRIGUE DOES NOT want to keep on going. That much is clear. There is no sound, but he's shaking his head like a man who knows danger. Like a man who has already lost something to danger.

The mic starts again with a 'Shit, man' from the cameraman, his Southern drawl reverberating with static and gunshots. He points the camera back and forth, from Rodrigue to the driver, who are yelling at each other in Sango. 'What the fuck, man?! Tell him to keep driving.' The driver seems to weigh up whom to listen to; the thirty-something Americans who will pay him in cash tomorrow, or the man who knows his language, and has used the word for 'kill' five times already. 'Don't stop, man, just go. Go!' The Jeep creeps forward a few feet and stops. Now the driver holds a mobile phone to his ear, but he's not talking. At some distance there is a rain of gunfire.

'What the fuck... Rodrigue: tell this motherfucker to start the car. Voiture. Commençer, voiture, you idiot. Tell him, Tim. We're missing it.' It takes Tim a second to get his mouth wet enough to speak. 'Dude, I think we should turn back.' Tim's knuckles are stretched bone-white around the driver's headrest. 'What do you wanna do, Tim: go back to the fucking hotel, and film some Evian bottles? Wake up nice and early to catch a presser? Fuck, man. What's wrong with you pussies?' Rodrigue, the fixer, looks at the road ahead and then at the road behind to figure out if he'll be shot in the face or in the back of the head.

The camera nosedives and extricates itself from the Jeep, attached to the sweaty palm of a thirty-year-old music video director from Tallahassee. Below the lens, the Central African dirt is fine and dry and orange. The cameraman lifts his machine and records Tim getting out of the Jeep, too pale in his pale-blue T-shirt, with its halos of sweat around the armpits and at the collar. Still arguing in French with the driver, Rodrigue follows Tim out of the car. 'No fucking reference. Moron,' says the man from Tallahassee to the driver.

The firing is closer now – minutes away. The camera is behind the other two; the fixer in his navy PRESS windbreaker, and Tim in his American Apparel T-shirt. There is something discordant about Tim, and it's not the fear. 'Tim, you gonna faint? You think you can tell us what's going on, here? You know, narrate this shit?' Tim stops and turns. He swallows his saliva and gags. Every now and again, the gunshots come with distant screams.

'So we heard reports of gunshots near the airport and—'

An explosion detonates streets away. A teenage boy runs out from behind a corrugated-iron hut and takes shelter inside a cabin across the street. He's followed by a woman and two more teenage boys. People start to cross the frame like ghosts, or extras. Two quick explosions and the camera is pointed at the dirt again. Mustard sand, now, and stones, their crunch underfoot picked up by the camera's mic. Gunshot makes the camera shake and slap against the mud wall of the hut beside them.

'Fuck. Fuck.' The cameraman runs behind Tim and stays close to his back; the camera picks up Tim's jeans. 'Walk fast,' comes Rodrigue's voice from behind. They are walking fast among tiny houses and shacks. The neighbourhood is deserted again. They turn a corner and see him. 'Oh, fuck. Fuck, man,' says the music video director. Tim vomits into the dust. Rodrigue walks over to the shape, followed closely by the man from Tallahassee. It's not one shape, it's two. Two boys. One dead. One bleeding to death from a red hole in his abdomen. 'Aidez-moi. J'ai mal.' Help me. It hurts.

Lois types the words into the text box. The red letters come up over the image, one after a bloody other. H. e. l. p. The full stop lodges itself in the middle of the hurt boy's torn-open knee. Lois pulls off her headphones and puts them down on the keyboard. Trapped inside the headphones, the cameraman's voice fades to a squeak. The lower third shakes with jeans and blood and subtitles. Lois rolls her chair back, but even at a distance things continue to unfold. The dead boy looks deader. The one who is still alive looks lost, delirious. (He is lost, she finds out around 4 p.m., two hours of footage later, when, on the back seat of the Jeep, the boy closes his eyes and death rolls them open again one last time.)

As the boys get carried off into the back of the Jeep, which has miraculously turned up, Lois looks around the room where she is working. There are eight computers, three of them in use. Two monitors to the right is a guy in a hat and parka. He appears to be animating the credits for a food or travel show, or maybe it is a travel food show. Next to him, a girl with long blonde hair watches a screen where another girl with long blonde hair and fast-moving lips fondles a leather handbag from a luxury brand.

Lois gazes back into her own monitor and hits the space bar on the two boys. They stop in blurry freeze-frame, as though some transport of the souls were already taking place. The two boys – who can't be older than seventeen or eighteen – fill the screen. Their moment in the sand is framed by the subtitling software browser, which looks like a navigational instrument. To the right is a text file of the words on screen, like a step by step to the end point. A path of subtitles from 'What the fuck, man' to two dead boys. Underneath, positioned in the ribbon of free space on the screen, is Lois's email, and the history of an earlier conversation with her mother.

'It's basically a castrated cock.'

'Ha.'

'I didn't want to do turkey. We just did the whole turkey thing.'

'Yeah. I'll take a castrated cock any day.'

'Yes, yes, Lois… Get all the capon jokes out of your system now.'

'Capon. He sounds like a superhero. Capon – the superhero castrated cock! A cock with a cape on it!'

The boy who is dead has a film of yellow dust halfway up his Adidas tracksuit bottoms. It is like the line of scum on the bathtub at Guernsey Street. The blood forms a tiny black puddle that soaks in or out of his shirt.

Lois gets up and walks to the communal kitchen, past the numbered editing suites. She takes a paper cup and loads up the coffee maker with a cartridge of Donut Shop Blend. As the coffee pisses out, she turns the corner to the toilets and locks herself inside one of the cubicles. The dead boy flashes into her mind, his open eyes the colour of sand. Lois throws up into the toilet, flushing as she does so to hide the sound of her retching. She sits with her back against the door, and the tears start to push out of her eyes. It is painful. Not the crying, but how difficult it is to.

Lois wants the fat, warm tears, the ones that streak your cheeks and leave trails on your shirt. The ones that make it feel like you are looking through a glass bottom. The ones that make your nose run. The ones that conjure up the furball of choke at the back of your throat. The ones that relax your jaw, and paint grimaces on your face that dig up dimples to catch the fat, warm tears that caused all this shifting of skin in the first place.

Instead, all she gets are the needling, dry tears that don't get rid of anything. And the worst thing is, she has to keep reminding herself of the dead boy, because his face keeps getting replaced with Nick's.

But Nick isn't dead. Nick is probably home from work by now, packing for France, where her father is busy being unfaithful to her mother, who will soon be trussing a bird with no balls.

So why is she crying? Because she doesn't want to go home to Nick. Because Nick, for all his forgiveness and gestures, has stopped making sense. They are living it out, these days. And she wants the boy to live. The baby to have lived. She would leave Nick to bring them both back. And all her want is, ultimately, a great waste of energy.

*

When it is 4.39 a.m., Maya opens her eyes and stares at the black giraffe guarding the bedroom door. By 5.33 a.m. the giraffe is no longer a giraffe, but a wooden chair with Cole's blazer folded over its back.

Maya looks up at the wall across from the bed, where three ribbons of blue light from the chinks in the curtains are beaming onto framed pictures of her family. Cole's right eye with eyebrow, her father's crossed legs, Cole's sister's chin, tilted, another one of Cole's eyes, Gitsy's baby teeth – the light from the street gives them up in little morsels, like clues.

The biggest clue, perhaps, is the wedding picture. Cole grinning in a fine grey wool suit, Maya beatific in a long white skirt with a fitted rose point-lace blouse. They are sitting on the stone wall, legs dangling over the dwarf crab apple trees. Behind them is the Brittany house, with bouquets of white hydrangeas pinned to the blue shutters. Later that month, Cole gets a job in Geneva, working for the UN. They come home. Joan is delirious – she cried as she waved Maya off to university, and now Maya is back. Three years later, Cole gets a job in DC. Joan is happy for them. Happy there is someone in the US to keep an eye on Lois. In this wedding picture they are young and radiant. Six years on they still look as young as they did in the photo; two bodies on the right side of time.

Maya listens to Cole's breathing and, for a moment, tries to align her respiration with his. She falls asleep this way.

When it is 6.58 a.m., Maya wakes up again. She tries a meditation exercise she read about in *Marie Claire*, and falls asleep this way.

At 7.20 a.m., Maya is woken up by thoughts of Liz. When she is done thinking of Liz, she turns her head to the left to make sure it is still Cole who is lying in bed next to her.

At 8.02 a.m., Maya turns off her phone's alarm, due to come on at 8.15 a.m., and gets out of bed. She pulls on her sweatpants and goes downstairs to the kitchen.

The stairs are carpeted. Everywhere is carpeted. The carpet was put down by the previous owner to make the house more attractive to prospective buyers. The carpet is too thick to be tasteful, and it's white, which is just silly. Already around the dining table there are crusty puddles of orange pasta sauce, tears of dried apple juice and Cheerios glued to the pile. They've spoken of removing it once Finn is walking, but now Maya isn't so sure. She knows she's meant to want the wooden floorboards, yes, but now she's grown used to treading on the ridge of the step, and it feeling soft under the arch of her foot. Gitsy says it's like walking on fluffy sheep babies.

Maya goes over to the French doors with the kettle, to empty yesterday's water out in the garden. She knows yesterday's water is still potable, but it's a habit. New water for a new day.

The living room is white. White carpet, white walls, and a green sofa with white cushions and a white throw. On the walls there are two paintings by a rising Kenyan artist. Cole brought them back with him in April, after a three-week consultancy on governance and transparency in Nairobi. One is mostly white, the other is white with a transparent

47

grey geometrical shape in the middle. Finn's bouncy chair is parked in the corner, filled with the toys she and Cole picked up off the floor last night.

Cole's ability to work a ten-hour day, get in an hour of water polo, and still have time to be a devoted father amazes her. Frank never had the consistency of a Cole. Maya has no recollection of him ever giving her and Lois a bath, much less playing Rapunzel on the top bunk. Frank's strength as a father was in grand outings that were devised to be memorable. Not in the small stuff, which took place again and again, and was routinely forgotten.

In the week, he usually appeared just when Joan was about to serve dinner. They'd be sitting on the bench with wet hair and clean pyjamas, and suddenly Frank would come in the front door and take his place at the head of the table. After dinner, he would read his book on the sofa or wait for Joan in front of the television. The children would single-file down the stairs one last time to collect their goodnight kisses from him.

Weekends were different. Frank worked most Saturdays, but was with them on Sundays. There were weekends when he doled out his parenting from morn till midnight, with the same cultish ardour he directed at his research. Maya remembers him rousing them at the crack of dawn to go mushrooming. He filled baskets with plastic bottles sawn in half, and gave them each a pocket knife. They stayed out all day, came home with cuts on their fingers and teary from exhaustion. At night he turned the harvest into omelettes – one omelette per species of mushroom. Dinner would be ten omelettes, which came flying out of the kitchen way past the children's bedtime. If they found berries too he would let them make jam with him until they were too sleepy to stand.

Other Sundays he disappeared into his study with his books and maps, or took long sitting naps with his mouth wide open.

Maya looks at the white staircase that leads up to where her children and husband are still asleep. She walks over to the bookcase, which is filled with photography books and monographs but almost no novels, and feels for her phone on the top shelf. Two unread messages from Liz.

I'm writing a list of all the phenomenal things you've said and done so I never forget them.

I miss you already. You have warm, cinnamon skin that's never sweaty.

Maya smiles at the second message, and puts the phone in the pocket of her sweatpants.

She fills the kettle at the sink. It's a much better kitchen than the one in the rental apartment. Before they became homeowners. There's a breakfast nook. Cole always sets the table for breakfast the night before, and Gitsy's Hello Kitty cereal bowl is sitting next to two coffee cups. Empty and ready to receive.

When Joan stays with them, she gives Maya Ican'tbelieveyouhaveitthisgood looks. It's just empty coffee cups, thinks Maya. But she knows it isn't.

Maya takes the coffee out of the freezer and drops three scoops into the cafetière. Then she adds a fourth. She changes her mind, and dredges up half a scoop. She always does this – hesitates over the amount of coffee to put in. She leans against the work surface as the kettle comes to a rattle, and looks at the calendar on the fridge. Looking at December this way, a grid of seven possibilities repeated four times, the month falls into two categories: chaperone and liar.

There was Finn's ten-month check-up, Gitsy's ballet recital. Then Cole's mother, who came over from London to help out with the kids that week Cole was away. There was a dentist visit for Cole, and a hair appointment for her, and then all the SWIMMING she did this month. All that SWIMMING with Liz. SWIMMING in Liz's apartment, on Friday night, Saturday, another Saturday, Thursday, Sunday, Thursday night, and then last Monday. All that coming home with wet hair, but never smelling of chlorine.

Maya reaches above the fridge for the ready oats and tears the top off a sachet. She props it up against the toaster and takes out a small pan. She eyeballs a cup of milk and puts the pan on the smallest burner, holding it steady and stirring the milk just short of a boil.

Maya sprinkles cornflakes into Gitsy's bowl. A few scatter

around the bowl, but she leaves them there. She does not decant the milk into the little blue jug that says 'Kisses from Brighton', but instead sets the carton down on the table. Behind her the kettle screeches.

Maya pours the boiling water into the coffee pot and empties the sachet of ready oats into the little red pan, stirring it with a wooden spoon that has a leather cord looped through the handle. Today she finds this detail infuriating. If some objects are purely utilitarian and others only aesthetic, then everything in Maya's kitchen is exactly halfway between the two.

She turns off the heat and leaves the oatmeal to stand. She pushes the plunger down into the coffee pot slowly, imagining the suction is a black hole that could absorb all this whiteness in a heartbeat. She pours coffee into Cole's 'Paw, Yer Coffee's Ready' mug, and opens the fridge to get the cream. There is no cream, so she uses the milk that is already on the table.

Maya walks back up the stairs, past the front door with its stained-glass half-moon that is raining turquoise shapes onto the packed suitcases in the hallway. She walks into her bedroom and kisses Cole on the forehead.

'Paw, your coffee's ready.'

'Hmmm.' Cole turns his head and pushes his forehead down into the pillow. 'Your phone was beeping all night. Who the hell texts you at 1 a.m.?'

Maya pretends not to hear. After all, his mouth is full of pillow.

She puts the cup down on the ledge above the bed and goes over to the children's room. Finn is awake and sucking on his dummy. He looks like a big grey frog in his romper, kicking away at the bars of the cot. Maya wonders if Finn takes after her father – if Frank's legs were always so restless, even as a baby.

'Mama.' Gitsy's voice is buried deep inside her duvet.

Maya scoops Finn up into her arms and walks over to the top bunk.

'Good morning, darling.'

Gitsy kicks off the covers and pushes her forehead down into the pillow. Apart from her temper, Gitsy takes after Cole.

'Are we going to sleep on the plane?'

'Yes, you're going to have a long sleep on the plane.'

Gitsy sits up in bed and frowns at her mother.

'You said I could watch a movie.'

'You can, darling.'

'Then I won't sleep.'

'OK.'

Gitsy gets out of bed and sits on the white carpet of her bedroom, rubbing the sleep from her eyes with her little fists.

'Will it be today or tomorrow when we see Grandma and Grandpa?'

'It'll be tomorrow night.'

They are flying to Paris just to spend half the day with Gitsy's godmother. It seemed like a good idea back in

October, but today Maya isn't so sure. She wishes Cole had talked her out of it, but as ever Cole let Maya plan everything, reserving his contribution for the execution stage. He will drive them down to her parents', while Maya plays I Spy with the children.

'Then I'm going to keep my pyjamas on.'

'You can if you want.'

Gitsy pushes past her and stomps down the stairs to the kitchen. Maya takes Finn back to her room and lays him down next to Cole. She goes to the bathroom and starts the shower running. She closes the door and texts Liz.

Are you awake?

She thinks of Liz asleep. She's never seen Liz sleep – not properly, not through the night. A small wave of panic laps over her, enough to send out a discreet army of pins and needles to her brain. She wonders if this is what Lois means by 'anxiety'. Lois talks about anxiety as though it were a normal thing, a daily phenomenon. Where Lois has panic attacks, Maya writes to-do lists. It was ever thus.

The shower sounds like a great crashing waterfall. Maya remembers the advice she read in *Marie Claire*, and brings her breathing to the forefront. She closes her eyes. She imagines she is breathing in water. She imagines that watching Liz sleep is like looking at kindness itself, if kindness were sharp, and wise, and irresistible.

The breathing exercise is not working. The pins and needles

are bouncing up through her skull, and there is something cold and painful behind her eyes. Maya feels like she's being consumed by her vision – as powerless as a gulp of water. She sits down on the floor of the bathroom and leans her head back against the white tiles. She makes a note to put her phone on silent. The door handle goes up and down. 'I'll be out in a minute,' she says.

There is nothing to do today but go home.

*

She came over alone, in the spring. Back when they had Simon sleeping in the crate. In the days of equipment and training. They acquired the dog in January. He was almost finished being a puppy, but still they were convinced they had to get all this equipment. Different bins for different biscuits that would do different things to his nails, tonsils and hair. Brushes for his tail and brushes for his coat. A brush for his teeth. A metal stand to lift his food bowl up by seven inches. Things for him to chew on that made him feel like he wasn't allowed to chew on things.

By February, they figured out that he would eat most of their food waste, which suited them all. He did have to whine for several nights to lose the crate, though, which was humiliating.

He came to them via a breeder who lived in the mountains behind La Clusaz. He was a mountain dog for one whole year before Joan brought him home in the back seat of her car one evening. She was giggling like a child all the way home. She kept looking at him in the rear-view mirror and saying, 'Oh my God what have I done.'

It was painful to remember how, in the early days, they had him wearing a dog seatbelt.

The first one Simon met was Wim, the youngest. Wim lived in London. He came home from university every couple of months for the holidays or for reading week, or when he'd run out of money. When he was home, Simon's walks tripled in length and frequency. With him, he didn't have to submit to so many arbitrary restrictions either. Wim didn't seem to care when Simon jumped into the lake to swim in the reeds, and he let him chase the horse behind the supermarket. Simon had never understood why the other two took umbrage at either of those things.

He'd never met the middle one, the one with the children, although much had been said about him meeting the children. He was not to jump/he won't jump. He was not to bark/he never barks. And he was not to go bounding up the stairs if a little one was going up or down/he obeys commands very well.

Lois called in March to say she'd be home for their birthdays later that month. Joan and Frank were born one day apart. This year they had a party for Joan's birthday, but skipped Frank's. Joan said after the phone call that she was worried that something was up between Lois and Nick. Frank said that it was hardly unusual for Lois to make a last-minute plan to visit. Joan said, 'Maybe, but it's the first time I've thought the opposite of she's-too-good-for-him.'

'What's that, then? That he's too good for her?' Frank said.

'No, that they're perfect for each other.'

'I don't think that's the opposite,' said Frank.

Joan was convinced that Simon was good for Frank. He could be good for them, but only if they decided as much. The goodness was quite out of his hands. 'What if Lois decides I am good for her?' thought Simon. 'What then?'

He'd never met Nick.

He could tell Joan was concerned, but she was also excited that Lois was coming home, because this was the daughter who looked like her. Simon had noticed that there was often something ineluctable between a woman and the daughter who looked like her. It was the same with bitches.

They had him groomed for the occasion, and paid extra to have his teeth cleaned. Joan vacuumed his coat with the pet nozzle, and rotated the covers on his dog bed. The only other time they had him groomed was after he bred. Not before, mind – after.

On the day Joan went to pick up Lois from the airport, Frank and Simon walked down to the cheese co-operative. They took the shortcut across the field, Simon ruining his blow dry in the tall grass. Frank, whose heart sometimes went racy on these walks, spent a fortune on his daughter's three favourite cheeses: Beaufort, Tomme de Savoie and Saint-Félicien. When they got home, he tasted each one of them and gave the rinds to Simon. Then he sat down in front of the news. Simon thought about what he should do when she arrived, how to make the best first impression.

Whenever he thought he heard the car he got up, and Frank said, 'Down.'

They said 'Down, Simon,' in a way that betrayed their eagerness for an overabundance of energy. When they said 'Down' what they meant was, 'Why aren't you bounding more, you mountain dog? Show off that fabled agility of yours, won't you? Disprove the long-held belief that pedigree dogs have terrible joints, because some of the people we respect the most will judge us for not getting a mongrel.' And so he performed. Usually, he'd prance about a couple of times and look interested. He let them say, 'Down, Simon,' so that they could show off how well he listened and obeyed. That was one of the ways in which they made each other happy.

Simon heard the car pull into the garage. He got up and followed Frank out of the TV room. Frank said 'Sit' and went down to fetch his daughter's bags.

It was the smell that got to Simon first. He could smell her from the kitchen. She smelled like salt on a rock after the ocean has licked it, like the burnt bits at the bottom of a frying pan, like an older woman's cologne with butter, like wet human hair after the rain, and old leather boots ankle-deep in berries. Any berries.

As she came up the stairs, he could tell from her footsteps that this one wouldn't objectify him – that if they ever stepped out together, it might well be him walking her. He could hear her talking to Frank, and her voice was unmelodic but thrilling, and tired, and agitated, and warm but difficult at the same time.

He walked from the kitchen into the hallway and stood under the light, on the black marble compass rose that Frank had lugged back from Carrara like an expensive joke at Joan's expense. ('So what if the bathroom window is a sheet of plastic, I gave you the floor of a palacio!')

The brass door handle went down with that awful grinding click it was prone to when it was damp outside, and as she came through the door, which swung shut behind her in the wind, she looked at him and said: 'What the fuck are you staring at?'

*

They had always loved a challenge, and liked to think of themselves as a family that existed outside the time allotted. Waking the three kids at 3 a.m. to climb a mountain with sleeping bags to meet the sunrise, heaping three tired children into the back of the car at 11 p.m. to be rained on by some exceptional shooting stars, chasing sunsets like zombies after a long day of swimming in the ocean – these were the kinds of things they did to themselves as a family.

They did these things in a scrappy way, in a spirit of over-compensation. Joan packed picnics that became charted in the collective memory and were given epic, delicious names. That-time-mum-made-apple-and-apricot-turnovers-at-2 a.m. The-one-where-we-had-champagne-and-that-salmon-tart-in-the-shape-of-a-sun-in-the-middle-of-the-night.

Frank's job was to get the kids to the bathroom and into the car. Once upon a time, Joan relied on him to help get them dressed in the morning, but that stopped after he sent Maya to school one day with a hanger still in her sweater. In those years, Joan and Frank bickered about everything that was easy. Money, which they had enough of. Holidays, which they had plenty of. Each other, which they most definitely had. But during these feats of familial rallying they held hands on the gear shift, made out in sleeping bags under meteorites, smiled when the other spilled coffee in the sand or forgot to bring cups for the cider. And the children complained, and Maya cried, and Lois asked why they couldn't be like normal parents, who let their children sleep at night, and Wim was living proof that you shouldn't disturb a sleeping baby, and still Joan studied the tide timetables, and read any report that had something vaguely astronomical about it, and Frank loved that she did.

One night Frank promised his family the whole of the

Milky Way. Joan, who had been more or less ignoring him for three days over the latest late tax payment missive, snapped out of her resentment. By the time all five of them were in the car she was curling his coarse black hair behind his ear, and telling the kids a story from before they had them. Frank leaned his head into her hand, like a dog leans into his master.

When they were halfway up the mountain Lois asked her dad to stop the car and vomited in the woods, which were dark and terrifying. It felt like vomiting over the edge of the world, she said, when she got back into the car. Frank asked her to expand on this thought, which only made her want to vomit again.

They arrived at the Col de la Forclaz just after eleven. Joan and the children stayed in the car listening to the Milly Molly Mandy storybook cassette tape while Frank set up their family camp: a tarp and all the duvets that had been ripped off the beds and stuffed in the boot. By the time he was done the kids had fallen asleep again, and had to be carried one by one up the hill. Frank and Joan buried their brood deep into the nest of quilts and pillows, to where their warmth could bounce off the covers and off each other and keep them cosy.

A hundred yards to the left of them was the wooden jump that hang gliders used to launch off over the lake. Higher up in the pasture was the square brown chalet that opened as a snack bar in the summer. Below them was the mini-golf and the shed that sold postcards and souvenirs. The landscape was familiar, even in the dark.

They were warm together under the Galactic Centre. The girls whittled off the names of stars and constellations they remembered, and made up new ones. Joan flexed her fingers through Frank's, and squeezed them tight with every baptism. The sky was like a second lake. In the valley below, the real lake beckoned like a firmament with no end. Frank explained again what a black hole was. They all rolled their eyes, and even though it was pitch-black Frank said, 'I can sense all my women rolling their eyes at me. Do you all think I'm a boring old man?' And his women giggled and said, 'No,' and piled onto him, and crushed him down into the blankets, in the grass, probably in some cow shit, because they'd stared at the stars long enough now, and it was time to fall asleep like other families, those whose parents didn't rouse them in the middle of the night to chase a phenomenal sky.

Being in the dark on a mountain with his family silent, Frank felt the elements of his happiness come together. He forgot to think about foremen and plasterers, and unsolved problems of an etymological nature. On nights like these his ambitions for the family did not cause stress to Joan. On nights like these they respected him as much for his intellectual fibre as they did for his paternal abilities. And all this in the shadow of the mountains he'd scaled and been tamed by as a young man.

In the morning, when the girls woke up, Wim was in his mother's lap, a big quilted cocoon with only his amazed little eyes peeping out and that balky hair whorl slap bang on his forehead. 'We were looking in the wrong place, girls,' said Joan. 'That's the centre of the universe right there, on your brother's head.'

Frank lit the small gas stove and prepared an astronomical quantity of hot chocolate, which he traditionally made from a whole bar of chocolate. They dipped buttered bread in it, and watched the last of the night's shadow slink across the lake and vanish into a crack on a rock face. They were all alone on top of the mountain, soldered together by experience. They had just created one more discreet memory – to add to the eleven sunsets, two Perseids and four sunrises they'd already watched, clan-like – and in so doing had touched the future.

On the drive back down to the house the kids yelped in every hairpin bend, and already, the challenge accomplished, the mood was on its way back to normal. Like the part where you undecorate the Christmas tree. Now it was the adults who were tired. The two producers in the front seat had done their job. There was no hand-touching on the gear shift. The car was no longer a magical vessel. In fact, when it had refused to start in the fuzzy-damp dawn, there had been a brief argument.

They were approaching the line where the mountain officially becomes the valley when Frank slammed his foot down on the brakes. 'Did you see it?' he yelled. The kids looked out of the back window, hoping for a deer, or a bunny, or something out of a fairy tale. Joan looked anxious. 'What?' she said. 'Hang on, I'm going to get it.' And with that, Frank jumped out of the car and ran back up the road like a madman.

The kids watched in the rear-view mirror as their father jumped over the ditch and climbed up the ridge to the treeline. They watched him scratch at the ground, like a dog looking for a bone. 'What the hell is Your Father doing?' asked Joan. Lois knew to interpret the difference between your father and Your Father.

'I think he found a mushroom,' said Lois. 'You've got to be joking,' said Joan. Presently, Frank came walking back to the car with a long green stalk that was budding flowers the colour of buttercups. The clump of soil around its roots rained dirt over the car seats. 'Look at this,' he said. 'Isn't it beautiful? This is the most beautiful thing I've ever seen in my life. Even more beautiful than my children.' Lois giggled. Maya decided her father was joking, and joined in. Wim reached out for the alien plant with his fat little baby hands. Joan asked if he could pleasenotgetdirteverywhereinthecar, and didn't talk much for the rest of the drive.

When they got home, Frank and Lois looked up the plant in Frank's mountain flora encyclopaedia. It was a weed. A majestic weed called a Verbascum. Its leaves were soft like Lambs' Ears, and the flowers shone like buds of yellow crêpe paper. Frank planted the Verbascum in the back garden of the rental house, two feet away from the salmon-pink bone-shaped paving stones. They had just moved into their temporary home in the suburbs. The one they agreed not to unpack for.

By the time Frank's new house was ready to move into, three years later, the adored Verbascum had spawned a mighty weed army that tore up a quarter of the terrace and staged a hostile invasion of the neighbour's garden.

*

You're too good to be true.

Maya was walking through the departure lounge with Gitsy at her side and Finn strapped to her chest, looking for a toilet. Gitsy ran off ahead, but before Maya had time to yell at her to stop, she got sidetracked by a display of sweets.

'Can I get a lollipop?'

'No.'

'Why?'

'You just had breakfast. You don't need a lollipop.'

'I *do* need it, for my ears. They're going to pop otherwise.'

'No.'

'That's why they're called that.'

When I saw your neck in that last photo, I got all achy and thought of the word succulent. When are you coming back again?

'Do you want me to have no ears?' asked Gitsy.

The 30th, typed Maya.

'Can I?' insisted Gitsy.

'No,' said Maya. 'I already said no twice.'

That long? I think I need a cold shower.

I'll send you more pictures from France.

Maya grabbed hold of Gitsy's hand and marched her to the toilet.

Do it now.

What category?

Finn swatted at the phone with his fat little hand, and when Maya pulled it away he thought she was playing a game with him.

More jugular.

Hang on, I have to change Finn's nappy.

Maya unlatched the plastic grey changing table, which came down with a familiar thud and one of those dependable, scratched-out koala face stickers. She put Finn down on the table and held him with one hand while she pulled a nappy out of her bag. Gitsy was opening the doors to all the cubicles and slamming them shut.

'Gitsy, stop that.'

'But I want to find a nice one.'

'They're all the same. Just go to the toilet.'

Finn turned his head to look at his sister.

'Now, Gitsy!'

Gitsy stamped her foot, stepped into a cubicle and locked the door.

'You don't need to lock the door.'

'Yes, I do.'

'No, you don't.'

'Yes, I do. What if someone comes in and sees me?'

'No one's going to come in.'

'How come you always get to have privacy and I don't?'

Maya changed Finn and stood in front of the mirror with the baby resting on her hip. She pulled her shirt down over the collarbone, and angled Finn so he wouldn't be in the frame. Click went the camera.

'Why are you taking a picture?' asked Gitsy, from inside the cubicle.

'I'm not. Hurry up.'

'Are you taking a picture of the toilet?'

Three of Finn's tiny pink sausage fingers were visible in the left corner of the picture. She put the phone on silent, and sent the picture to Liz anyway.

'Are you nearly done, Gitsy?'

'No.'

Maya looked at her face in the mirror. The neons made the blue bags under her eyes bulge, and revealed tiny lines that made her lips seem pursed even though they weren't. Her arm looked distended and a bit too flabby from this angle. Finn pulled at her hair, and started crying when she pulled his hand away.

'Hurry up, Gitsy. Your brother's hungry.'

'I'm done. You can wipe my bottom now.'

Maya tried to open the door, but it was locked.

I miss you already. Don't go. Come to Turkey with me instead.

'Unlock the door, Gitsy.'

'I can't stand up. You have to wipe my bottom first.'

'Yes, Gitsy, I need to come in for that.'

'Can't you do it?'

'GITSY OPEN THE DAMN DOOR.'

Gitsy opened the door. 'Why are you always yelling at me?'

Maya moved into the cubicle, Finn bawling his eyes out on her hip. His little body continued to resist her as she wiped Gitsy, who went to push the flush.

'Don't touch it, Gitsy, it's dirty.'

'But I'm going to wash my hands.'

Gitsy tried to push down the lever and Maya yanked her back.

'What did I tell you? I can do it with my foot.'

She pushed the flush down with her boot and followed Gitsy to the sink. Resting her knee against the sink, she balanced Gitsy on it so her daughter could reach the tap. She lathered up all six of their hands and held them together in the warm water.

'Now my sleeves are all wet.'

'It's just a bit of water, Gitsy, it'll dry.'

'No it won't. It'll never be dry for France now.'

She went to find Cole, who had picked up two coffees and

was reading the paper at their gate. It occurred to her that reading the paper was the very last thing you did, a reward activity to crown those times when every other task was completed. Maya put a now-screaming Finn on her lap and unbuttoned her shirt to feed him. Her phone vibrated.

I'd like to slide my mouth up and down your perfect neck and suck on your earlobe.

Finn latched onto her in that detached way babies have of draining you.

Like a lollipop? she replied.

Cole kept on reading the paper and ignored Gitsy, who was crawling back and forth under the blue plastic airport chairs and knocking into people's ankles. Cole looked unflustered, like the man who has it all. Finn sucked fanatically on his mother, closing his eyes to the glaring airport lights.

If you didn't stop me, I would suck the life right out of you.

4. Green Carpet

WHEN JOAN AWOKE on 22 December, she could feel her children on their way to her. Maya, Cole and the kids were probably in Paris already. Lois and Nick would be leaving later that day. She wasn't sure when Wim would arrive, but he lived in London, and since they shared a time zone his trip felt more like a commute.

Frank was out with the dog, and the house was as still as it was clean – a necessary foundation for chaos, thought Joan, taking a sponge from the sink and wiping the coffee ring from the kitchen table before it tattooed the wood. After she did this, she realised the coffee ring was the only crooked item in the day, and that everything big on her list was already scratched off. Today she could attend to small messes in a vacuum of other, grander messes. And then her children would arrive, and nothing would matter anyway.

Frank had stacked some logs in the basket by the wood stove. He must have chosen the logs carefully, because they were all the same width and length. She stopped to wonder if this was something Frank was likely to have done – consider the appearance of the logs in the basket, or, better still, consider her observation of the appearance of the logs in the basket. She decided the uniformity was a matter of chance.

Joan finished Frank's tepid coffee and swept some pine needles up from under the tree. Another easy fix. Later in the week the tree would rain its needles onto the floor, but they would be too loud and too busy being a family to care.

The tree was a perfect blue-green cone with fat, moist needles. The tip of it was a foot from the ceiling, barely enough room for the blinking star Lois had made in Year Seven woodwork class. Joan walked back to the kitchen and unscrewed the top of the steel thermos they made coffee in. She emptied it into Frank's cup, and went to the fridge to get some milk. There was something slightly obscene about how full the fridge was.

Yesterday, at the supermarket, she saw herself feeding each member of her family individually, with love. She bought endives and little cardboard baskets of overpriced greenhouse berries for Maya and the children, salami, brown-sugar biscuits and cornichons for William, and quenelles for Lois. She bought the things they said they missed on the phone,

not really thinking about how it would all come together –
thinking only of her little girl and how big her eyes grew when
a plate of little white sausages of pounded fish smothered in
red sauce was put down before her.

Joan closed the refrigerator door and walked over to Frank's
office, with the intention of fetching the boxes of photos. His
computer was open on the desk. She sat down at the desk and
opened Frank's history *Eldena Ruins with Bakehouse and Barn,
Hünengrab im Schnee, Morning in the Giant Mountains, Mann und
Frau in Betrachtung des Mondes*. It was all Caspar David Bloody
Friedrich.

She opened up his email and signed in with the password
he thought she didn't know – 'GrandesJorassses' – his trophy
climb as a young mountaineer. She saw the H folder – the only
folder – in the left column and knew it contained everything
she needed to hate Frank. The idea of hating Frank right
now, with the children on their way, seemed exhausting and
senseless. Instead, she went to the drafts. She knew that the
truth was mostly hesitated over. It came from the head, from
the heart, but seldom got sent.

None of the drafts had subjects, apart from one. It was a
question.

Dubai?

She clicked open the message. It was empty, save for the
subject line.

She tried to recall the last time Frank had asked her a

question. It was yesterday. He'd called and asked if he should pick up bread on his way back from walking the dog. She tried to remember the last question he'd asked that wasn't food- or errand-related. 'Do we have to?' They'd been invited to a Christmas party by one of Joan's expat friends. It was an annual gathering of the town's British contingent that Frank tried to get out of annually. He had no interest in standing around a piano singing carols, and found the food at these things barbaric. Joan didn't want to go either, but welcomed any excuse to separate Frank from his computer and drag him screaming into the folds of civil society.

'I don't know what to say to any of them,' he ventured.

'Oh for God's sake, just ask after their children,' said Joan.

Carols? Baguette? Overdraft extension? The Truth? She slammed the laptop shut and walked over to the walnut wardrobe with its hammered-gold rivets and marquetry stars.

The wardrobe was wonky and its constellations uneven. They'd bought it at a flea market in Brittany, and driven back to the Alps with it strapped to the roof of their second second-hand VW, before the kids. They continued going to Brittany after the kids were born, renting rooms in farmhouses on the same adored stretch of the coast. One morning, so the legend goes, Frank drove to the village to get croissants and came back with a farm of his own. He bought it for pennies on the pound from a woman keen to liquidate her ties to the region after a failed affair of the heart. Thus one woman's tragedy became another family's bliss.

The starry wardrobe was filled with relics, spares and spare relics. Fondue pots, a box that had once contained a bottle of whisky now filled with mismatched knitting needles, a sewing box that had belonged to Frank's mother, chipped mugs that needed Super-gluing, a marble Viking chess set from the 1950s and several shoeboxes of photos.

Joan removed the biggest box and brought it into the living room. She emptied the box onto the table and scattered the photographs gently with her hands. The children looked up at her from the table with their toothy grins, summer freckles and mosquito bites. The older version of these children, she thought, had nervous breakdowns and passports that needed expedited renewal, and even children of their own who looked up at them.

Each picture boiled down to a pair of gingham catalogue-order shorts, a melting ice cream, a sunburn, a plaster cast, a certain vintage, a long-deceased bunny, a wasp sting. They were as deep as a museum diorama, and they threw up years that were over – good years that remained, but no longer existed. She picked up the photos one by one, bringing them close to her face, and then dropping them in one of three unmarked piles: one for Lois, one for Maya, one for William.

Among the photos of the kids was a black and white picture of Frank, wearing tiny mountain shorts and hiking boots and posing in front of a stony ridge. His red backpack leaned against a rock, against which was also propped a bottle of wine. Frank was smiling straight at the camera. His body was tanned and muscular – every inch of it exuding youth and confidence in his surroundings. Joan tried to coax the memory out of the mind vault of hers and Frank's shared history, but couldn't. Perhaps that German woman had taken the picture. She took it to the fridge and covered with it a photo from Lois and Nick's wedding party.

The phone rang.

'Hi, Mum.'

'Wim. I was just looking at you a minute ago.'

'Hmm?'

'Sailing camp, in Douarnenez. You're sitting on the side of a Sunfish, and you're so cold your lips are blue.'

One year, in Brittany, they enrolled the kids in sailing camp. The children launched their dinghies from the same stone ramp Frank had used as a child. They went out into the bay on tiny boats, circling an island that was inhabited by a lonely cow. Legend had it that her calf had tumbled off the cliff and drowned, and now she haunted that same spot, mooing madly at the waves.

Frank and Joan hadn't had that much time alone in years. They spent it walking along the harbour, avoiding the squished sardines that slipped through the crates to be pecked at by gulls. If it was raining they sat in a café with newspapers and magazines. That was back when there were no mobile phones, no instant connection to anyone but themselves, and the pages of magazines smelled like Guerlain perfume samples. Whenever she walked into a newsagents, Joan breathed in that new magazine smell to fan those holiday memories and keep them alive a little longer.

Brittany? Maybe she'd send an email to Frank with that as the subject line. It occurred to her only now that, in buying the house in Brittany, Frank had reconstituted a chapter from his own childhood. He wanted once again to flit between the ocean and the Alps, only this time without the in-between, high-rise poverty. She imagined the look on his face if she sent him an email titled *Caravan holiday in Cornwall?* God forbid they ever reconstitute any chapters from her history.

These days they only spent a week in Brittany every year, often without any of the children there. Joan suspected that Frank now saw the blessed disconnection he'd sold to them years ago as an inconvenience. Maybe they could go there in March, and make fires. She made a mental note to arrange for the chimney to be swept after Christmas. She'd oppose any plans to install Wi-Fi.

'I finally got round to sorting the pictures.'

'Yeah?'

'Remember, I said I'd give you each your photos.'

'Kind of.'

She wondered if he was eating properly. If he was struggling to keep up with his classes. If he'd run out of money, and was too embarrassed to ask.

'When are you arriving?' she asked.

'Tomorrow. I'm coming on the train. Probably get in late.'

Would he like the blue sweater she'd bought him for Christmas, she wondered, or would he rather have the money? She had kept the receipt somewhere.

'Hey, Mum, can you do me a favour?'

'Yes.'

'Can you look out of the window and see if there's a red Volvo next door?'

'Just a minute.'

Joan walked over to the kitchen window and pressed her index finger on the counter to pick up some crumbs.

'Yes. Is that Tara's car?'

'Yes.'

'Oh, lovely – she's home too, then?'

It was still strange to think of Tara as Wim's girlfriend. It seemed like just yesterday she'd caught them in the pantry, eating from the Nutella jar with spoons. Like just yesterday she'd picked up payphone calls from Wim, trying to renegotiate another school night curfew.

Just yesterday, in fact, Joan had watched Tara's father nail their fake, spray-painted Christmas wreath to the front door. Tara's mother was standing by him, arms crossed in the morning cold, overseeing the installation like it was the relaunch of the Hadron Collider. Joan had found the scene amusing. She wondered if Tara's father also had a woman he was secretly writing to, and if Tara's mother was the kind of wife who would smash her collectable Danish plates if betrayed.

'Why are you doing that to the pictures?' William asked.

'So you can each have your share.'

'Share? You make it sound like it's an inheritance.'

'It is, isn't it?'

'I don't understand why they can't all just stay in one place.'

No one ever said it, but they all considered her the Keeper. She was the one who filed away the kindergarten macaroni art, kept the children's birthday cards in separate folders and memorised the family tree so that twice-removed Sicilian cousins on Frank's side could be put into context as and when needed. She was the one who carried the burden of keeping everything in One Place.

Frank's indiscretion got her thinking about turning One Place into Two. Or rather, his indiscretion had added value to the idea that she might be better off living without him, somewhere else – a thought that popped up as reliably as the mole that tore holes in the lawn every spring. But up until now, the thought had been born of an abstraction – the itch of any marriage, the tedium of the everyday realisation that nothing ever changes, not even the foolish hope that it might. Now Frank had actually given her a reason to upend their lives. And if a move was on the cards, the preservation of the family archive would have to become a shared burden. Was that why she was sorting the pictures? She wasn't sure.

'Call us when you're on the train.'

'I will,' said Wim. 'I'll text Lois.'

'See you tomorrow, darling.'

'Bye.'

Joan took three big envelopes from Frank's desk and labelled them with the children's names. She finished dividing the photos, faster now, and took the stuffed envelopes upstairs. She laid them out on their beds, which were tucked in neatly like hotel beds.

She thought of the thousands of times she'd roused them from their beds in the morning to get them ready for school. When they first moved to the new house the girls rejected their newfound privacy and slept together for almost a month. In the mornings she would find Maya and Lois coiled around one another in Maya's bed, tangled up in those cold, unclear fears that age only makes clearer and colder.

Frank and the dog would be gone for another half-hour, she hoped.

Joan went to the bathroom and started running a bath. She took off her clothes and stood in one of the warm patches she knew how to locate, where the underfloor heating actually worked. She wiggled her big toes inside her sweatpants and walked her eyes up her legs. There were some barely noticeable ripples around her knees, which looked softer now than ever before. She had good legs. Had always had good legs. 'Chi ti chiama gorgeous?' an Italian boyfriend once asked her. 'Scommetto tutti ti chiamano gorgeous.'

The same Italian boyfriend used to rub the crotch of his Levi's with a wire brush so that they might look used there. What was he doing now, she wondered. He was probably married. Perhaps he was having an affair, too. Perhaps she could find him and have an affair with him. She wondered how other women had the confidence to let themselves be desired.

The bath was almost full and the bubbles were like a thick coat of icing on a wedding cake. Joan looked at herself, and saw that there were parts of her that hadn't changed in years. The flesh on her thighs was softer, perhaps. Her arms, too. All this softness that eroded your angles with age. It was enough to harden you. She looked at her tummy. The kids had not given her stretch marks, but they'd stretched everything else that was stretchable – including her forbearance.

Frank had never made a secret of his desire to be alone, obsessing over one thing or another. For years he carried a notebook in which he scribbled thoughts of a botanical or architectural nature, collected questions and listed topics for future research. He dawdled in bookstores, dragged the children to the library at the weekend, and generally pursued a great many interests he seldom shared with anyone. In time, the notebook became a laptop connected to endless avenues of fact and, instead of his signature vanishings, Frank became known for his infrequent apparitions. It was the difference between being an escapologist and just not being there in the first place.

That was the thing about obsessions, thought Joan, applying a green clay mask to her face. They start off as silk thread and end up a cocoon. Frank had woven a cocoon around himself. He could see through it, breathe through it, eat through it, and every now and again fuck through it, but no one had any idea really how alive he was in there.

Downstairs the front door opened and she heard Frank call the dog in. She wondered for a moment if she had forgotten to log out of his email, and then decided it didn't matter if she had. 'Who's a good boy?' said Frank.

Not you, thought Joan.

Joan stepped into the tub and reviewed the fights that were about to be had. Maya and Lois would bicker about the bedrooms. Or rather, Maya would make assumptions about which room had been allocated to whom, and Lois would pretend not to care, but throw tiny daggers about other things. Lois and Wim would fight because they were so similar. Everyone would yell at Frank at some point, and he would feel besieged. Maya would stage a one-person intervention for Frank's benefit, and would get upset when it was her feelings that got hurt. Probably, no one would fall out with her, she thought, but Lois might make her feel pathetic.

The bath was stinging-hot, the French postal service had promised to deliver the last of the presents she'd ordered tomorrow, and the kids were on their way. Almost on their way.

*

Lois spent her last hour at work putting subtitles under a Catholic priest in Bangui. The priest was running a mission house, which dispensed first aid to Catholics and Muslims alike. He insisted on this point. She copied his thoughts about God's children and the new dispensary, and how peaceful life was before people started shooting and hacking at each other with machetes, and pasted them at the end of a text file called The Warlords Love Poetry Project.

She'd started on this project soon after landing the subtitling gig. It was a way not to be left with just the truth, which was blunt and bloody, and had a body count. She chopped up the subtitles, the translated words and sentences of generals and foot soldiers, and reassembled them into love poems. The more sentimental the better. She took army and militia chiefs, UN peacekeepers and aid workers and turned their strategies into sweet nothings. The priest offered some good staples – words like 'brother', 'love' and 'surgery'.

Two years ago she had embarked on a similar exercise with travel plaza reviews left by the public on Yelp and other ratings websites. It was her way of digesting Americans – those foreign creatures – by compiling what they wanted for their cars and bellies, their leisure and personal hygiene requirements, and then organising it into verse. It was the ultimate act of translation.

'How will you ever get used to them?' Frank asked Lois, when she made it clear she wouldn't be coming back to France after her MFA. That summer, Joan, Frank, Maya and William travelled to Fishers Island to see Lois be married off by a priest. The church ceremony was followed by an unceremonious piss-up at Nick's parents' house. Later, Nick's father pulled out his nautical charts for Frank.

Packing up her things tonight, Lois thought of the hawk spitting hairballs in Corona. She took out her phone and typed a to-do list of things to achieve before she and Nick left for France the next day. She'd failed to get anything for her sister's children, and wondered if there was something that could be procured without leaving the neighbourhood.

Last year, everyone had received a copy of her chapbook: *Yelp Travel Plaza Review Poems*, published by Incomprehensible Womb press. Her parents had been supportive in their own ways, that is to say, in ways that were diametrically opposed. Joan had said, 'You're so clever,' and Frank had typed out a line-by-line critique of her work. Wim ordered copies at every bookstore in London, giving a fake name and phone number each time. Maya never said a thing. When she visited her sister in the spring, Lois found the chapbook in Gitsy's room, covered in doodles and *Frozen* stickers. A further translation, she thought.

All writing – like all relationships – was a matter of combining. An arrangement. To hear the Historian speak, there was nothing left to his relationship when he met Lois but the reciprocal servicing of individual agendas. The working marriage was rolled out at the PTA fundraiser (her), at champagne receptions they pretended not to care about (he), but the brutal honesty was kept for lovers, girlfriends, workmates, and also for the creative and intellectual confessionals provided by their work (she was a dancer with a big New York company).

As she exited the building, Lois checked the Historian's Twitter. She did that every now and again, searching for signs of domestic misery on social media, and feeling relieved when she found none.

'She tells me she stopped all communication like she wants a medal,' Nick told the marriage counsellor they had started seeing, back in the spring.

'It's common for spouses or partners to try and negate the attachment left over from the affair,' said the counsellor. 'There is usually a phase of abnegation.'

Lois kept her mouth mostly shut during those first sessions, for fear that more unnecessary truths would come dribbling out. The sessions provided an audience for her guilt and a witness to Nick's magnanimity. They never quite got to the part where the cheating party considered why they'd had an affair in the first place. In fact, they stopped going to counselling the moment they regained a certain equality in their sessions – an equality Lois thought Nick was not ready to concede.

On her way home, Lois picked up a bottle of wine and a bag of peanuts, and stopped in at the Chinese dollar store. She bought a plastic Statue of Liberty with infra-red eyes for Gitsy and a cat clock that spoke the time in Chinese for Finn. She knew her sister would confiscate them, like she disposed of all carcinogenic plastics.

Nick was home, wrapping books at the kitchen table. He'd stopped at The Strand on his way home from work, like he did every year, and bought everyone two books. There was also a bag from the Natural History Museum, where Nick worked, which she imagined contained age-appropriate, non-toxic gifts for Gitsy and Finn.

Four years ago, Nick landed a job writing copy for the museum's education department. He spent his days writing child-friendly descriptions of rock specimens, outer space, life groups and dinosaur bones. Once, when the Historian scoffed at this, Lois felt like slapping him. They had the same job, she and Nick. They rarely brought anything new into the world – they merely transformed what was already out there so that specific groups of people (say, francophones, or the six-to-fourteen-year-old demographic) could access it.

They had tried to bring something new into the world, once. But that particular collaboration flopped when the foetus gave up at three and a half months. This event ushered in a deep bout of depression for Lois, which only started to lift when the Historian approached her after her sloppy wedding karaoke rendition of 'Kiss Off'. 'I make it my business always to seek out the most interesting person in the room,' he said.

Once, she asked him what would happen the day they walked into a room with a more interesting person than her in it. 'Not going to happen,' he said. He gave good answers to questions, the Historian. Other times, the things he said were disastrous. Like after their first kiss, one morning, by the charred stumps of Pier 56. By any measure it was a chaste kiss. It could still have been written off as an awkward brush caused by an overabundance of sunlight. Could still have been made not to count. But that wasn't going to happen. To Lois, the kiss felt promising and dangerous – like tampering with history. 'That wasn't even a kiss,' he texted her later that day. 'Just two people catching their breath.' What a lie. If anything, the kiss sent them both into a state of apnoea and panting want.

Lois dropped her bag and put her arms around Nick from behind, to feel him in any way she still could.

'Don't look,' he said. 'Your presents are in this pile, too.'

'I won't.'

She emptied the peanuts into a bowl and opened the bottle of wine. She poured two glasses and gave one to Nick.

'I got offered some work over Christmas,' she said.

'Yeah?'

'Yeah. I got an email today about subtitling an old war film.'

'Which war?'

'The first one.'

'You know World War One wasn't actually the first war, right?'

That Nick could still joke about history was a good sign, she supposed.

The offer had come in from MoMA that morning. It involved translating into English the title cards of a 1928 silent docudrama called *Verdun: Visions of History*. The film had been discovered in some dusty, near-abandoned vault in Moscow, and was to be shown in the new year with a live cello accompaniment. Lois wondered whether the gig had anything to do with the Historian. Had he passed on her name? And if so, had he written it in an email or said it out loud? Had he used her full name or just Lois? And if so, how did that feel? Did it feel like regret, or like history?

They watched the first forty-five minutes of the film that night, in bed. After almost an hour of dead boys in trenches and black and white blasts tearing up the French countryside, Lois noticed that Nick was fast asleep. She closed the laptop, laid her body flat alongside his and shut her eyes.

86

*

'You were grinding your teeth all night,' Nick said the next morning.

'It's because we're flying,' said Lois, picking at the leftover peanuts while Nick made coffee.

'You can do that thing where you pulverise my hand for seven hours to make yourself feel better if you want.'

'I might just do that,' she said. 'I might also do that thing where I take a pill.'

After breakfast they each cleaned one side of the house, and Nick brought down two weeks of recycling. In the street, a taxi honked. Lois looked at their apartment, clean and quiet and pre-abandonment, and, as she closed the door on it for a fortnight, wondered how much longer she'd be living here, and in what capacity.

*

The interviews were numbered from one to twenty-two. One: militia men. Two: random soldiers. Three: Catholic priest. Four: bush militia. Five: MSF Six: general. Seven: more soldiers. Eight: medical student. Nine: paediatrics nurse Ten: Muslim kids at airport. And so on, all the way to twenty-two. Of the twenty-two, twelve were interviews of fighters. Men in battle fatigues with amulets and oxidised machetes, and lots of very young boys. Lois clicked on the first subtitle file, which bloomed open into three different windows. As she hit the export button, to keep only the column of words, with its timecode anchor, the plane groaned. Nick turned his head to her to remind her with his eyes that planes always groan before take-off.

Lois reached into her pocket and brought out the two-dose corner of Xanax she had cut off earlier. She popped open a blister and swallowed one of the pills. File one had finished loading, and her laptop whirred from the extenuation of the task. Nick squeezed her hand, which was sweet, but prevented her from opening file two. The titles from the first file occupied her screen in a tragic column:

Turn around.

What is it you wanted to show us?

There was shouting everywhere.

They tried to cut us up.

We answer only to the people.

We are all volunteers.

We are all volunteers.

We have no representatives in government.

Lois hit Select All, changed the spacing to single and centred the words, turning the column into a pillar. A flight attendant asked her to put the laptop away for take-off. Soon the plane started its taxi down to the runway, making Lois wish she were on firm ground in Queens, anywhere out of the window, instead of in this unlikely machine. Nick opened his book. The plane was rushing down the runway, gathering speed. Lois closed her eyes and leaned her head back against her seat. Nick took her hand in his again without lifting his eyes from the paper. She heard the pages as he turned them. Each page sounded like: 'Flying is a thing I, unlike you, can do without being devastated.'

The plane climbed up with the noise of a tin can whizzing down an airshaft until it reached an altitude it liked, and started purring like a good piece of equipment. Lois felt parts of herself unclenching. Soon, Nick fell asleep.

As the plane zoomed towards Nova Scotia, Lois turned the warlords into lovers. The fighters wore amulets, small wearable temples made of beads and string, to protect them from sharpened machetes and stolen bullets. Lois turned them into love talismans and gave them new powers. She'd started off by turning the militiamen and war strategists into men who wrote love poems; romantic aubades before the battle. Turning hate speech into declarations of love. Diplomacy into lovemaking.

Now she started listing the complications of love: missing, frustration, lying, impossible juncture. Cheating. She found that the words of these men lent themselves better to love's red flags and dead ends, its dashed incitements and unfair power.

She wondered who would meet them at the airport. If her mother had volunteered her father for the job, he'd surely be late.

We are all volunteers.
We are all volunteers.

*

'Isn't there a hole I'm meant to be watching out for?' asked Cole, as they came up the driveway.

'Yes, it's when you get to the maple.'

'I think we passed the maple.'

'No. I don't think so. Just stick to the left.'

'The civilised thing would be to have one of those lights that comes on automatically when you come up the driveway.'

'It's my parents, Cole. Just be thankful the hot water's working.'

'We don't know the hot water's working.'

'You're right,' said Maya. 'We don't.'

After Cole got the job in Geneva, they moved in with Joan and Frank until they could get on their feet. Within six months they found a furnished one-bedroom apartment on the French side of the border. For those six months, having a fellow countryman in the house brought out an accent in Joan that was unrecognisable to Maya, and had been long forgotten by Frank. Overnight, Joan became indefatigable on the topics of England and her childhood. She made Sunday roast for weeks, until they all asked her to stop. Joan's exhumation of her roots came as an utter surprise to Maya, who looked on it with some suspicion. Joan felt it, and for the first time ever enjoyed the sensation that she was different from them all. Perhaps to meddle with his wife's new allyship, Frank put himself in charge of his son-in-law's integration. Cole's induction to the French Alps was historical, semantic, gustatory and unrelenting. Their shared interest in her new husband brought Maya and Frank closer than ever before, and during that time they achieved a peace unwitnessed before or since. Cole, however, was happy to stop touring cheese cellars every weekend, and when he and Maya moved into the new apartment they did not extend an invitation to Joan and Frank for two weeks. 'You can be overbearing with your passions,' said Joan. 'Only to you, Saint Joan,' said Frank, wondering if there was some truth in her vision of things.

Cole stopped the car by the curtain of bamboos, which even the headlights couldn't pierce. Beyond them lay the gaping jaw of the swimming pool, empty but for a couple of feet of water that would turn fetid in the spring and be a-jump with toads.

'Do you think there's ice on the pool?' asked Cole.

'I don't know,' said Maya. 'Can you carry Gitsy up the stairs?'

'That thing is like the 9/11 memorial.'

'I don't feel like talking about the pool right now. Can you just get Gitsy upstairs?'

'Yes. Jesus. Relax.'

Maya bristled at the word. It wasn't that his instinct was

wrong, it was just that when he told her to relax she felt as detached from him as a ledge does from the man who trips off it.

Cole opened the door on Gitsy's side and extricated his daughter from the car seat, untangling her long brown hair from the seatbelt. Gitsy folded herself over his shoulder, gripping his jumper with her sleepy hands. Maya followed behind with Finn and the nappy bag.

'Are we here, Papa?' Gitsy asked.

'Go back to sleep, darling.'

'But I want to pet Simon.'

'You can pet Simon in the morning. It's very late. Everyone's asleep.'

'Is Simon asleep?'

'I'm sure he is.'

Maya and Cole walked up the steps to the house with their floppy children. The house at night looked like a cross between a bunker and a Dutch canal house – all impossible angles and candlelit slits flickering in the dark. Maya stuck to the wall and away from her father's vertical rock garden, which in the night, and without a guard rail, seemed like a bad joke.

Joan opened the front door. Maya knew she must have been looking out for them. Must have seen the light come up from behind the hills and snake in and out of the next hill, vanishing and reappearing between the barn conversions and new builds. Each one of them had looked out for someone that way: boyfriends, visiting cousins, Frank/Dad…

The living room was trembling from the fat church candles Joan had lit, and the heat from the wood stove carried a sappy smoke into the hallway. Maya kicked off her shoes. The light had always been butter-yellow in this house. No matter the bulb or the atmosphere, the lights here never burned cold white like they did in some houses. Maya mouthed 'Hi' to Joan, and nodded 'Yes' to her gestured question of 'Tea?'. She walked up to Lois's old bedroom, with its boat bed and cot, and laid Finn down.

'Don't pet Simon until I wake up,' Gitsy ordered Cole, who was pulling off her shoes and socks.

'I promise,' he answered, tucking her fully clothed into her aunt's childhood bed.

After Cole left to fetch the bags from the car, Maya crossed the corridor into her old bedroom and sat down on the bed. There was an envelope on the pillow with her name on it. In it were a bunch of photos of her as a child. She took her phone out of her purse and turned it on. The phone woke up and whirred a few times as it caught up with the time zone. A message from her phone provider telling her she was in France and six work emails she didn't care to open showed up on the screen. She wondered what Liz was doing that was preventing her from writing. Probably sleeping.

Maya took off her socks and pressed her toes into the

carpet. Outside, Cole triggered the light on the neighbour's front porch, and the glare flooded the bedroom, painting Maya's toes white, like boiled bones.

Maya looked for Liz in the shadows of the room. The children would wake up tonight because of jetlag, and she would have to deal with it. Stopping in Paris had been an absurd idea. Downstairs, in the kitchen, Cole laughed at something her mother said. Maya found Liz's nose in the curtain pole, the back of her head in the shadow cast off a lampshade. She looked for Liz's shoulder, which she liked to use as a shelf for her chin when they lay down next to each other in bed.

There had not been much sex since the birth of Finn, an enormous baby who had catapulted himself into the world with such speed and determination that taking something to allay the pain of his arrival was not an option. Cole had waited instinctively to touch his wife, and even then doled out caresses that were so gentle and unassuming that they passed quite unnoticed. Maya didn't even notice they'd not started having sex again until months after the date at which they might reasonably have expected to want such a thing to resume.

Maya wasn't sure when exactly she had lost the will to possess Cole. It could have been on that walk to the George-town waterfront, back in July, when they'd bought soft-scoop ice cream, and Cole had put his hand on her bare knee, and she'd thought how odd it looked there. It could have been a month later, when she called Liz a week after the workshop and asked if she would like to meet up for a drink. When Liz said yes, Maya realised she didn't know where people went to have drinks. 'Anywhere that's easy for you,' she said. 'No, you choose. You're the one with kids,' Liz replied.

She'd invited Liz to their house the following week, wanting perhaps to lay it all out for her to see – the life she and Cole had built, with its modernist Danish furniture and school schedules, and just enough excess to feel like what you had sufficed.

It was a couple of weeks later that Liz kissed her. The kiss was like a question, beginning to end. In the next few weeks, Maya had seen her love-troops retreat. She stopped working on Cole and instead moved on to another fortress, one that looked like no other victory or collaboration before. But Cole thought of himself as still won over, was still in thrall to Maya's hawkish perfection and will, and she had kept up the ruse, throwing a shadow army at him to keep things ticking along, but deploying her strategy on Liz.

Maya lay back on the bed and pushed her hand down into her jeans. She left the hand there, and Liz walked into the room with a cup of tea, her wet hair wrapped in a towel. All of Liz's towels were those waffly cotton ones. She was one of those people who only ever washed whites with other whites. The towels always looked like they had just come from the shop. Maya sat up in bed and stretched her hand to take the cup of tea Liz had just made.

Maya wiggled up the bed and cupped her hand.

She was tired. Too tired to think of Liz in that way. She imagined Liz as a bed to sleep on, and her head fell to the side. Her mother would understand. Cole would talk to her mother, fill her in on the progress of the second bathroom renovation and how much Gitsy liked her teachers at Franklin Montessori. He would tell her mother that they didn't want the children spoiled rotten this year. No more than five presents each. Nothing that needed batteries. He'd show interest in the dog. Yes, he could be relied on and she could sleep, with her hand on Liz.

Maya lifted her phone up to her face and typed.

Don't make me go to sleep in a room with a green carpet without you.

She sent the message and her arm flopped down on the bed. She thought of how bad it would be to fall asleep with her phone on, wide open, with its 300 messages to Liz. Before she turned the phone off she wrote one last message. Liz's wet hair would leave a sopping halo on the pillow. The tea was a special blend of herbs Liz had come up with just for her. Gingko for her circulation problems and valerian for her unreliable sleep patterns.

Don't make me go to sleep in a room with a green carpet without you.

*

Last night I thought I would die
in the dust
without you.

My only desire:
to go up in flames
in that same old spot.

I have my papers to prove it.

Brothers and sisters
we were, back then,
(some details are classified)
before the fighting, before
I disarmed him.

Two people
in a room at the Sheraton
hacking away
hashing it out.

Men, women:
all of us volunteers.
All of us volunteers.

Spell it out for me:
I thought I would die
without you.

Lois hit save and closed her laptop. Nick was sleeping against the window, his mouth slightly open. His hand was between the two of them, open, even now. Lois rubbed her toe in circles on the pine-green airplane carpet. She imagined the Historian, Christmas shopping for his wife. She tried to picture him thumbing through bras and panties in a high-end lingerie store, but all that came up was a Historian-shaped blob, seen from the back.

In the end, nothing could soothe her like a note from him. He became a vocation. Once, he told her to meet him at the end of Pier 51. He left his office late, and sent a message from every block. Every message sent her into a silent panic that only made her heart more audible. *I've never been inside the Church of the Holy Apostles – have you?* And, *There's a stairwell on the corner of 22nd and 10th. I'd like to fuck you standing in that stairwell.* He made her sick with longing. He killed her appetite. His want was an added benefit that flavoured just about everything. *I'd like to get a room at the Jane, and go in and out of you all night like there's nothing else left to do.*

She tried to recall what happened when he finally got to the pier – how they kissed, if he pushed his fingers through the buttons and up her shirt like he sometimes did, if they remained standing, or if she sat down in his lap like she sometimes did. But the memory was vague, and her recollection of the embrace not as unctuous as she had hoped. Her mind kept switching back to the new, approximate vision of the Historian in the lingerie store until finally her old lover melted into the racks of bras and knickers, sending Lois into a fragile but welcome tranquillity, 20,000 feet above the ocean. There was nothing else left to do.

5. The Nativity Scene

OFTEN IN NEW YORK, Lois saw the Alps from her desk. She described it to Nick as a stroke of nostalgia, halfway between memory and a headrush. She'd be translating a pharmaceuticals catalogue or subtitling a video, usually with her headphones on. Her eyes would look out of the window and for a second of lost focus, the Manhattan skyline, behind the lesser, Greenpoint skyline, became the saw-toothed Alps.

To be precise: it looked like the view of the Alps she knew best, the one you had from the top of the mountain behind her parents' house – the same mountain that had been the backdrop of many a family nocturnal. If you looked east and squinted, the Alpine jag melted into a rickrack of eternal snow that blended blue rock into blue sky.

Coming through town, Lois and Nick got their first glimpse of real mountain. The drive from the airport had given them rolling hills and dips, but the peaks were only promised later, when you reached the lake. The town centre at midday was full of cars and people carrying shopping bags. The backdrop lake looked like unrealised ice. They passed the old condemned hospital with its red and blue windows, and went up into the foothills of the Semnoz to drive home the back way, avoiding the traffic of tourists on their way to the ski resorts.

On his first trip to the Alps – their honeymoon – Nick had followed Lois up and down the mountains and around the lake like a child follows a butterfly. Lois was that eternal child with a contagious devotion to the small and miraculous facts of life. He was tickled that a girl like that might want him. In fact, it made him giddy how much she seemed to want him. They broke into the playground of her old senior school and made out in the gymnasium, fucked in cinematic meadows and carved their initials on a tree. She slid her toes up his leg under the table, while Frank pontificated about biodynamic wine and Latin roots. She told him the place had been waiting for him, had been nothing but a vexation until he set foot in it.

It was his first time going back to France since the affair – back to the place where Lois was once a child, and not a person with the ability to murder his trust. It was also his first time back since the miscarriage. He worried that spending a week with her sister's kids – particularly Finn, with his drooling, fat-cheeked perfection – might be hard on Lois. The few times she'd brought up her uncertain, gloomy desire for a baby since the affair, Nick was disgusted with her. 'If you wanted a baby so badly, why did you fuck someone else?' or: 'Is it just anyone's baby you want?' Both of them knew, deep down, that there were two answers to that last question.

Today, driving along the back road to the family home and despite grogginess from the flight, Lois seemed upbeat. But that was the thing about Lois – she could go from butterfly to sinking stone in a beat. And the intensity went both ways. Nick sometimes wondered whether, when he'd met Lois, he'd mistaken her anxiety for energy.

Back when she was fourteen, Lois begged Frank to drive to school the back way, even though it stretched out the drive, because it went past the house of a boy she liked. Their statuses at school were inversely proportional – she was the half-English new kid who was too odd to bully, he was a semi-pro snowboarder two years older than anyone in his year. That he was the best-looking boy in school went undisputed.

It is not an exaggeration to say that the entire playground went quiet the day he walked over to Lois one break. At first, she suspected a prank. It turned out he wanted some Metallica lyrics translated into French. They hung out together again the next day, and the day after that. By day four his aura had granted her a certain immunity in the playground, and no one dared tease her about this irregular friendship.

One day he invited her over to his house after school. His parents were out. He took her up to his older brother's room in the attic and locked the door behind them. Lois closed her eyes, stopped breathing, and tried to make her mouth some version of kissable. Instead of kissing her, the boy walked straight past her to where a small, round mirror hung on the wall. 'Open your eyes,' he ordered. She did. He took the mirror down and flipped it around. 'See this?' he said. On the back were scribbled the word 'Ersatz', and underneath, 'Steffi, ich liebe dich.' Steffi was the German exchange student who lived with them. He put the mirror back on the wall, unlocked the door, and swore Lois to secrecy.

She had to wait another four years to be kissed, in the dank cloakroom of a nightclub called Sugar in a depressed university town in the West Midlands.

Lois pointed out the house to Nick, who pointed out that she'd already pointed it out six, and four, and two years ago. 'It's the same truck from twenty years ago,' said Lois. 'It's practically a historical artefact.'

There was no room behind Maya and Cole's rental SUV, so they parked at the foot of her parents' driveway. Frank was in the garden, holding two metal stakes in one hand and a mallet in the other. Simon stood by him, panting clouds of hot breath into the sunny cold.

Lois took out their bag, handed it to Nick, and slammed the boot so hard the dog winced. As they walked up the driveway

Lois picked up a stick, and Simon wondered if it was perhaps for him.

'What are you doing, Dad?'

'Making the garden safe for the children.'

Lois kissed her father on the cheek and Frank thought of the questions he should ask about her life, and the knowledge he should fold into said questions to prove he was up to speed.

'Is everyone here?' she asked.

'Your sister and your mother are up there, getting everything organised. I think your brother's coming tonight.'

'What is there to organise?' asked Lois.

She looked for signs of the emotional affair her mum had mentioned – something in his voice, perhaps, or his appearance. But Frank didn't look like much of a lothario. He looked like a man defeated, with his stakes and his garden full of holes, his mortal slopes and balconies deprived of guard rails. Lois could only imagine what shit Maya and Joan combined had given him.

'Hey, can I borrow some money and the dog? I'm going to go to the bakery.'

'Aren't you going upstairs to say hi to your mum and sister?' asked Nick.

'Tell them I'll be right there. I'll bring breakfast back for everyone.'

Frank took what he had out of his pockets and gave it to Lois. Lois looked at Simon. Simon walked to her.

'He doesn't need a leash,' said Frank.

'I know that,' said Lois.

Nick shook Frank's hand and continued up the steps. They were both thinking it: how come she gets away with leaving before she's even arrived? How come we all indulge this aloofness of hers, encourage her childish instinct to do whatever the hell she wants? And Frank: how come *she* gets to stand outside the circle without being yelled at?

Lois took her hard-fought right to oddsheep it down the lane with the dog.

'We don't have to talk,' she said to Simon, when they were out of earshot. 'We can just enjoy the last of the quiet, and I can share my crazy pass with you.'

Simon looked up to Lois, and as he did so his wet nose banged against her hand. She extended her fingers and scratched the side of his snout, which was damp from drool.

Frank went back to child-proofing the garden, and as he banged the first stake into the ground he watched his daughter and his dog walk away from his unsafe trap-of-a-house.

*

Simon had fallen in love with Lois in the spring.

There had been no acts of love, just the dull certainty of love, its titillating deadlock. He didn't know when he would see her next, only that until then days rolled into days, rolls rolled into rolls, and his eyes got dry from gazing into space. Seats that were once comfortable were now functional. Meals that tasted good were just matter. He lost his opinion about baths.

Simon knew this might very well be the last time he loved, and it made him feel like a one-worker factory. So many things to keep running despite this love crisis.

He was in love with a beautiful, brilliant woman and there were all these things he wanted to say to her, like: I want to eat your heart right out of you, I want to cock my head so I can lick the side of your foot – but all that came out of his mouth was woof woof woof woof woof woof woof woof woof woof woof woof woof woof woof woof woof woof woof woof woof woof woof woof woof woof woof woof woof woof woof woof woof woof woof woof woof.

*

As he watched his daughter – the one they all made allowances for – run off with his dog, Frank thought of Heide. She had no children, no dog, and he supposed she lived the selfish life of a twenty-year-old, only with more money, less time and assuaged ambitions. There must be no frenzy in her life, he imagined. He thought of how much room the woman had in her life for intellectual pursuit, and decided she must have chosen her current situation as a means to erudition. He felt old, bewildered and besieged. He envied and wanted Heide in equal measure, or, if the balance tipped one way, he couldn't be sure which.

Frank's affair was a jutting bone on a man who'd stopped growing. Heide, long hair flying in the wind out of the window of Frank's VW, was like a stunted-growth diagnosis. Joan was the healthy part of him – that time of the evening when his knee stopped jerking, the absence of an eye twitch, the invisible dickering in his blood once he'd taken his meds.

He had known her forty years ago. They met in Italy, the year before some mutual friends introduced him to Joan. It was in Trento, in the summer. It was the first time he'd ever tasted medlar fruit. She was hitch-hiking, he picked her up, and instead of dropping her off near Geneva as planned, drove her the extra 400 miles to her parents' house in Wiesbaden.

He stayed in Wiesbaden four days, sleeping in a youth hostel. He swam lengths in the narrow Opelbad pool while she packed up her life to follow him back to France. They returned via Freiburg, and Frank splashed out on a night at an inn in the Black Forest. He would return to the Black Forest three years later with Joan, on their honeymoon.

Frank and Heide joked that it was a long trip for a change of clothes, and compared notes on membership numbers in the youth wings of their respective countries' Communist parties. They lived together for nine months in Frank's one-bedroom apartment, on one of the pedestrian streets that moated the castle. They spent all their money at the market and in the German tavern by the canal. One day, when Frank came home from the office where he worked as a junior architect, Heide was gone, along with the things he'd driven halfway across Germany to fetch.

The abandonment had been painful, but lined with the utter certainty that new opportunities for love would present themselves. And Frank certainly had a love of opportunities. Particularly, opportunities for obsession. He met Joan that same year.

Frank placed two wooden garden chairs by the side of the pool and tied a rope between them. He knew they would disapprove. He didn't particularly want to anger his wife and youngest daughter, but the ease with which he could do so disguised itself in his mind as placation. He walked up the steps to the house with the shears, and on the way cut a few branches that could arguably poke a child's eye out.

Inside, Gitsy had hijacked the hallway for a wedding procession of Maya's old stuffed animals. The animals were wrapped in toilet paper and the bride's train was leaking its felt-tip designs onto the grey-white marble. Frank sat down on the step to remove his garden boots, which were shedding clots of earth onto Joan's clean floor. He thought of getting a dustpan to clean up the mess, but he didn't know where to find it, and if he asked Joan she'd be angry, which would defeat the point of pre-empting her anger.

Maya appeared with Finn sitting on her hip and chewing on her scarf.

'Oh my God, is it true you paid Lois to not come in and be normal and say hello to us?'

'She went to get croissants for everyone.'

'It's 11.20 a.m. We all had breakfast four hours ago.'

Joan came out of the kitchen and stared at Frank's muddy feet. Cole and Nick were sitting at the table, drinking coffee. For a second, he thought he should join them. Frank did not know what to talk to the husbands about. He would give himself until Lois came back to be alone, and then, he promised himself, he would think less of H and take part in the family.

Frank walked into his office and closed the door behind him. He noticed his email was open on the desktop and felt like vomiting. He logged out and then logged in again. He took his sketchbook out of the drawer and whistled for the dog. He remembered the dog was out with Lois. He wondered how Lois would handle Simon on the main road. The dog knew to stop, but you had to put your hand on his back to remind him. He'd neglected to tell her that.

It was Lois and Maya's idea to get a dog. Their argument was that, now that William was gone too, he and Joan would tear each other apart if they didn't have a third party to come between them. Frank said it was out of the question, and Joan reminded everyone that she hated dogs. The pressure built up for several months and Frank even wrote them a sonnet titled 'You Get a Dog', which he published on a blog created for the occasion. And then one night Joan had driven to her friend's chalet up in the mountain and spent an evening drinking rosé next to a litter of puppies. She was tipsy, and pissed off at Frank about the stupid house, and the fact that the glass door in their first-floor bedroom opened onto a fifteen-foot drop. She adopted out of anger.

And now Frank had a dog that followed him around building sites, and ensured that he stuck to the exercise regimen the doctor had prescribed for his heart. At first Simon learned Frank's tricks too quickly, and since there was no satisfaction in that for either of them he endeavoured to eke out his training, so that Frank might feel like the master of something.

The door opened slowly and Finn crawled into the office. Frank looked at Finn for a second.

'Dad.'

Maya came in and scooped up Finn.

'Yes?'

'Mum and I are planning to have oysters tomorrow, so we'll need you to shuck them.'

'I always shuck the oysters.'

'Don't you think it's weird how Lois didn't even come in to say hello?'

'Not really.'

'What are you doing?'

'Working.'

'Are you going to be in front of your computer the whole holiday?'

'I'm working.'

'Great,' said Maya. 'Whenever you two sociopaths want to join us, we'll be decorating the tree.'

The good thing about Maya's blame was that it got shared equally between him and Lois. Joan only had eyes for him when it came to resentment. Frank enjoyed being a witness to his girls' healthy rivalry. It was like a game they could play blindfolded: Lois provoked Maya, Maya coaxed provocations out of Lois. They infuriated each other in a vacuum of consequence – in the same way that disliking a part of your body is futile. They had argued about absolutely everything in their lives except the fundamentals. Frank assumed Christmas would be one long, loving joust between them.

He reminded himself to pay special attention to Wim this year. Wim sometimes got forgotten in the wake of his sisters' achievements or crises. As kids, the girls would spar for his attention, competing with fake tears for his snuggles and kisses. It usually ended with Wim in tears, overwhelmed with his inability to console both sisters at the same time. There was something extra-pure about that boy's heart, Frank had always thought. Something deeply allergic to unhappiness. In many respects, this worried Frank. He had difficulty imagining Wim in a managerial role, for example, or having to deliver bad news to anyone, ever. There was having a good heart, and then there was moving through life. He would talk to Wim.

Frank stood up and followed Maya downstairs, where the wedding guests now lay scattered to the whims of the Gitsy cyclone, their unravelled toilet paper trains torn to shreds all over the floor.

*

For many years, the piano room was just a room that was missing a wall and housed someone else's baby grand piano. It had been intended as the antechamber of a greenhouse: a boxed-in terrace that straddled a half-inside, half-outside concrete koi pond. But Joan, who had seen how frogs took over another of Frank's intentions – the pool – had stopped the project the only way she knew how, by wearing Frank's enthusiasm thin.

For the month during which they collaborated on the design of the French windows they experienced a romantic renaissance, and even though a new dullness had taken over since, Joan thought fondly about Frank every time she opened the door to step into the back garden.

The French windows overlooked the raw concrete pool, which, true to form, Frank had ignored long enough for it to become an element of nature. The order Joan created stopped at the glass door, and beyond it was all mounds of unclaimed dirt for a rockery, jutting iron rods to hold up invisible but vital structures, and yet another hole of submerged construction materials. In the cold, they looked almost delicate, thought Joan, as she flattened out the creases of a holly-green tablecloth.

Maya, Gitsy, Nick and Lois were decorating the tree in the next room. Finn and Cole were taking a nap upstairs. Frank had sat in the living room for twenty restless minutes, the spasm in his knee knocking up against the coffee table. Now he was back at his computer, tapping out statements to or about the Germans.

Joan fetched the bottle of port from the kitchen and put it on a tray with five tiny glasses. She stacked some mince pies on a plate and put those on the tray, too. At Christmas she kept a permanent tray of mince pies on the windowsill, wrapped in a linen dishcloth. She must have made 200 mince pies this year, and still she knew that wouldn't be enough.

'Look, Grandma!' said Gitsy, pointing to the wooden parachuting Santa. 'Mama said this was her favourite when she was a little girl.'

'Really? I remember your mama liking the fuzzy apples with the sparkly leaves,' said Joan. 'She used to lick off the glitter.'

'Your mama was a glitter-licker,' said Lois.

Joan put down the tray and fetched her Nativity box from the starry chaos cupboard.

Every year in December, Joan had signed notes from Lois and Maya's teachers, allowing the girls to join the class field trip to the town's expo centre, which had hosted the same touring Provençale Nativity scene since Joan first set foot in Annecy from England in the 1970s as an English-language teaching assistant.

How glamorous it had seemed that first summer. Drinking flimsy glasses of white wine outside a medieval lock-up, watching the tan lines build up between the straps of her gladiator sandals, all those neon geraniums... Being the only one who could sing along to the radio. And then that first winter. The beauty of this place under snow. The winking lights and chocolate shops in Chamonix, and the men falling over each other to teach her how to ski – all of these things made more exciting by the notion that here it was she who was exotic. To come all the way to the Alps for something else, only to realise that you were something else.

On the day of the field trip Joan gave the girls their allowance, which Maya would spend on mass-produced trinkets in the gift shop. Lois would save hers and deposit it in her New York coin bank – a carton of Weetabix with a picture of the Manhattan skyline glued across it. Nearly twenty years later, when she had just moved to Brooklyn, Lois found the box intact in her parents' basement. The 107 francs it contained in coins could no longer be redeemed for euros, so Lois flew the cash back with her and emptied it into the East River.

Joan, who was generally unmoved by French folklore, couldn't understand why the girls, who had seen the Nativity scene every winter from the age of four to ten, were so excited for the field trip. The idea of walking single-file around a crowded hall to look at hand-painted clay figurines depicting vanishing handicrafts like basket-weaving was not the kind of cultural exercise that made Joan tick.

The old ladies who lived in expensive lakefront apartment buildings came out in droves for the Nativity scene. They snaked around the hall oohing in their mink capes, reeking of mothballs. The matching rouge and lipstick, the auburn perms, their appetite for complaint as conversation... The people of this town – particularly its women – remained a mystery to Joan, who was known to use her from-awayness as an excuse not to participate.

Two years ago, the year Wim moved to London to go to university, Joan dragged herself to the Nativity exhibition to follow in the footsteps of her scattered children, and remember them that way. She wanted to watch other small children wind their way around the show like a pleased snake with many heads.

It was a revelation. Here was a world contained and still, dedicated to the preservation of memory. Of late, Joan felt that she had stopped the active production of memory that kept the family busy for the past twenty years, and tipped into the preservation beat. The figures were fixed, perfect and busy with discreet tasks that embodied not only their lifetime, but probably the lifetime of their parents. The children in the Nativity scene did not go off to America, where they subsequently had nervous breakdowns and no medical insurance. They did not choose to go to university in London and only pick up the phone when they were in arrears of rent. No – they stayed rooted to the spot and had a healthy Mediterranean glow, even in winter.

Joan unpacked the figurines she'd collected over the last two years, buying two or three every few months from a catalogue or online. The statues were packed in toilet paper and bubble-wrap. There was Jesus, Joseph and Mary, and three Magi from when the kids were small and they'd invested, as good parents do, in the basic supermarket Nativity scene. To these Joan had added a fishmonger, a woman with a bread stand, a woman carrying a tray of cheeses, the neck of a bottle of wine between her fingers, a basket weaver with real wicker props, a dancing bear with a cuff around his leg and his handler. There was a butcher with a necklace of sausages, a flower seller with small bouquets of lilacs in a basket, and a couple of young lovers who looked like they'd been plucked from a ronde.

The Nativity scene, like Joan at Christmas time, was all about labour. It was about surrounding Jesus with workers, drowning the foolhardy pursuit of heaven or happiness in the fishmonger's cry for fish and the mother's cries of pain.

She'd always remember the look on Frank's face when she pushed their first daughter out. It was a look of utter devotion and at the same time a picture of obsolescence. 'What have you just done?' he seemed to ask, his face struck with a look of awe. 'What have you just done to me?' was also a possibility.

Frank had never met his biological father, although he did have to sort through the man's possessions when he died in 1980, in a rented studio apartment in the South of France. 'He was proud of you,' said a neighbour. 'Proud of what you became.' Finding out that his estranged father had somehow accessed even the most basic of updates on his life and formed a positive opinion about it sent Frank into a deep depression that lasted the better part of two years.

Family, to a young Frank, was the number of kids to a bed, scratchy wool coats made from American military blankets, having to walk to school instead of taking the bus, and rationing. His own father had started off relatively rich, the son of a wealthy industrialist who made his fortune in yogurts and crème fraîche. He had left Frank's mother pregnant and penniless, and later been disowned because of his drinking and gambling. Frank provided for Joan and the kids with a vengeance, and in order to do this left for work before they woke up and often came home late.

Because he worked so hard, he afforded himself moments of selfishness, moments dedicated to the study of things that charmed him, like Hölderlin's poetry and the names given to French bogs. But to the others, the time spent at work and the time spent in study merged to form a single block of absence, so that Frank became mysterious, even to his own kids.

It is true he compensated for this with his wild moon chases, foraging expeditions in the autumn and a whole week of presence in the summer, when he took the kids shrimping and fishing, and cycling, and swimming – often past the point of exhaustion.

Once, Joan managed to convince Frank to see a shrink.

'Tell me about your father,' the therapist asked, on their first appointment.

'I don't have a father,' Frank said.

'I guess we'll start there, then.'

Joan blew dust off the brown crêpe and artificial-moss barn, and placed baby Jesus in his too-orange manger in the centre. She put his virginal mother beside him. Like Jesus, Frank had been a prodigal son. Joan unwrapped the last of the figurines, looking for Joseph. Like Frank's father in the months following the birth of his son, he was nowhere to be found.

With her Nativity scene as complete as it could be, Joan started to arrange her collectible, hand-painted French workers into semicircles around Jesus. For fun, she moved Mary out and replaced her with Boules Player Jeanot. She stood Mary beside the butcher, with his blood-smeared apron and his stand of sausage links. The woman with a marrow on her head she paired with the wise man, and turned them so that they had their backs to baby Jesus. And so Joan formed her union, from the ground up to the heavens.

In the next room, Gitsy was putting all the baubles on one branch, which was drooping so low it almost touched the floor. Maya was busy rearranging the decorations, spacing them out and tucking the fairy lights deeper into the branches.

Last night, Joan had caught herself thinking that maybe, just maybe, her heart wasn't in it this year. Women in magazines wrote about that time they didn't do Christmas but found cheap flights to Madeira instead, or just read a very long book. She'd banished the thought from her mind, and reminded herself that they all relied on her. That family milestones don't just mark themselves.

Even Frank, who at times seemed to want to write her out with his self-isolation, needed her. He owed her his life more than the kids, she thought. Without her, Frank would live off bread and cheese, and become one of those hoarders you see on television. He would surround himself with maps and books and mountains of hi-res printouts of German paintings, until even his children would stop visiting him.

The tree was decorated. Cole plugged the blinking star into the garland of fairy lights. Gitsy clapped as it winked white and then gold. Finn looked at his big sister and joined in the clapping.

*

As long as they remembered, there had been a poinsettia at Christmas. The poinsettia must have preceded the joke about there always being a poinsettia at Christmas, but no one could be sure.

This year there were two poinsettias – one blood-red, the other white. There were also bowls of nuts in their shells, painted nutcrackers with cotton-wool beards, and red and green doilies that only came out in December. Lois envied her mother's ability to make a Christmas, to excel in the categories of food, decoration and gifts. She recognised the same ability in her sister, although Joan was her own workforce, and Maya tended to outsource. Joan had always been an executor. Maya delegated or procured. Either way, the yule log turned out perfect.

Lois rubbed a velvety leaf of the white poinsettia between her fingers. Next to her was a bottle of wine Frank had brought up for her earlier. It was one of Frank's concerns that Lois and Maya did not have access to good wine in the US. It was one of Joan's concerns that Lois drank too much. Lois drank her glass clean and went to pour another. She sensed Maya tallying how many drinks she'd had from across the room.

She had assembled two more poems that afternoon, shrinking her source material. The main difference between these and the travel plaza poems was the topic of death. Aside from the odd hyperbole about service station coffee, death was largely absent from travel plaza reviews.

Last autumn there had been a reading of her chapbook in a bar in Bushwick. Nick and the Historian both showed up. As Nick negotiated the strange room and a world that was his only by invitation, Lois felt the Historian's advantage. He mingled as though a poetry series were his natural habitat. When Lois read he stared right at her, communicating with her still. After the reading Nick stepped out to smoke, and the Historian purchased one of the chapbooks. 'Dedicate it to me,' he ordered, opening it up at the title page. And she had. The next time she met the Historian was one of the few times they had sex. Introducing a little bit of Nick into the equation had made their situation a little more untenable, a little more desirable.

This book, Lois decided, she would dedicate to Nick. The previous book had been a trick; this one would be an exercise in salvation.

Men, women:
all of us volunteers.
All of us volunteers.

Spell it out for me:
I thought I would die
without you.

Joan had gone to bed at the same time as the children. Frank was in his office, writing about the structure of branches in

Friedrich's work for his blog. Lois had spent the day looking for more signs of her father's affair. It was shocking to think that, underneath his predictable front, the quiet routine of his trademark obsessions, Frank was moved to love. Again. If anything, Lois noticed, her mother seemed less affected than normal by his need to retreat to his office the minute dinner was over.

Cole was catching up with work in his bedroom, and Nick had fallen asleep in front of the television, watching *The Shop Around The Corner* dubbed in French. Simon was sitting at Lois's bare feet. His fur covered her toes, and when she nudged him in the ribs he purred like a contented cat.

'Don't you find it weird,' Lois asked Maya, 'the way Dad tries to get him to do tricks for us?'

Maya put down her magazine and came to sit at the table.

'Why is that weird?' she said. 'It's what people do with dogs.'

'I don't know. It's just, he never did that with us, so why would he do it to his dog?'

'What – ask us to fetch?'

'No, I mean, show us off, make us perform for people. It's like he's unlearned how to raise kids.'

'It's a dog, Lois.'

Simon rolled out the tip of his tongue so it would touch Lois's big toe. He could taste her woollen sweat. The taste of her zipped through him like the smell of food.

Lois poured Maya a glass of wine.

'No, I'm OK. I'm not really…'

'What, you're not pregnant again, are you?

'God no,' said Maya. 'But I'm still breastfeeding. Well, kind of.'

'Oh, right.'

After the miscarriage, the doctor told Lois that motherhood had only been postponed. That there was always a reason. That a healthy, viable baby would be on its way in no time. But the fact was, she wasn't getting pregnant.

Lois had asked the doctor how long before she could start trying again for another baby. 'That's a question for you and your husband to answer.' The answer came back, blatant and unhelpful. She was talking about risk, but all the doctor seemed interested in talking about was feelings. Feelings were a risky business, too. But statistics, probability, dates, time codes, diets, studies… there had to be evidence. She wanted to know whether it would happen again. If there would be another pill to fetch from the pharmacy, delivered in a white paper bag, along with a tube of hand-counted Vicodin. If she'd have to call her mother again to have a conversation that ended right then and there, one of those stupid talks that has nowhere else to go. 'The body bounces back, Lois. What we need to make sure of is that your mind…'

Lois saw her mind bouncing up Fifth Avenue, towards Central Park; a gelatinous clear blob shaped like a water balloon that jumped from car to car in slow motion. People in offices looked out as her mind waltzed past their windows, light and supple and visible to all.

'There's this theory that you can't get pregnant by someone if you're emotionally engaged with someone else,' said Maya.

Lois was familiar with this theory. Nick had said the same thing after he found out about the affair. He also called her crazy, and said it was fucked up to want to get pregnant while she was carrying on with someone else. Wanting a baby overlapped with wanting Nick's baby, but that wasn't the whole story. 'I have this fantasy of getting you pregnant,' the Historian told her once. It was possible that, by calling it a fantasy, he had jinxed the whole thing. Later, she hated him for that.

'Who are you emotionally engaged with?' Lois asked.

'You're going to be shocked,' said Maya.

'I doubt it.'

Lois pushed the stem of the glass closer to Maya.

'Have one. It's Christmas. One bottle of formula isn't going to affect his chances of getting into an Ivy League school.'

Maya scowled at Lois, and travelled the glass the last foot back to her. She picked it up and drank.

'So, who is it?' asked Lois.

'This woman I work with. Worked with.'

'Oh.'

'See? You're shocked.'

'No. I'm just shocked it took the gender expert eight years of practising gender expertise to figure out she liked women.'

'I don't like women.' Maya paused. 'Just her.'

Simon was snoring under the table and giving Lois a cramp in her left foot.

'I'm telling you because…'

'I know why you're telling me.'

'Why?'

'Because you've thought of telling me so many times since it started that by now, blurting it out is just a formality.'

'You think you're so clever,' said Maya.

Maya had always been the beautiful one. She hadn't grown up with the anger of Lois, who burned easy in the summer and had been slamming doors since she was ten. Maya had olive skin, long brown hair, long black eyelashes, and didn't look as if she had to be negotiated.

'Does Cole know?'

'Of course he doesn't know.'

'Are you going to tell him?'

'No.'

'No?'

'No.'

'Why?'

'Because if I tell him, I know he'll forgive me.'

While she was still on the wrong side of Cole's understanding, Maya felt her life might still change, that she was still a mass of possibility, a ballot not yet cast.

Lois and Joan had from the start envisaged Cole in the abstract, and known that whatever alliance Maya made would be forged in mutual strength and healthy good looks. There was going to be no time given to flailing in this marriage. Cole and Maya were late university sweethearts. They'd both gone through the people who were almost as promising as them but not quite, and their love was touching and efficient, a deep-running partnership. There was always respect there – the kind that Lois and Joan looked at suspiciously and with some envy, but with a realistic lack of ambition.

Maya's problem today was not that she was cheating on Cole. Her problem was that in his romantic temperance and soft spot for those who fucked up, he denied her the last drop of agency in her own nihilism.

'So who is this woman?'

'She's called Liz.'

'Liz what?'

'I'm not telling you.'

Lois thought of telling Maya about the Historian, about how she, too, had crushed and been crushed more than was decent. She considered warning Maya about how shitty all this would look when she realised that the end of that love was written into its very existence, and how there would be no painless exit when you most needed one.

But it was Maya's moment, Maya's cataclysm. Lois was in a different phase now. She had been forgiven – or almost. Maya was in love in the present, still out in a storm of her own making. Lois was back inside, in a room with a man who thought he still might want to, perhaps, be loved by her.

'How did you meet?'

'At a workshop on gender violence at my NGO. She ran it. She lives half the time in DC and half the time on this farm, her grandparents' farm, in West Virginia. Mum would love it – it's that kind of place.'

'Wow.'

'What?'

'It sounds…'

'What?'

'So different from what I've always thought you wanted.'

Maya breathed a sigh of relief.

'Now you tell me a secret,' Maya asked her older sister.

'I don't have any.'

'Of course, you do. Everyone does.'

'Not really.'

Lois wondered whether to tell her sister about the curse of their family, that shared restlessness that had made her, Frank and Maya look elsewhere for what they felt the universe owed them. She thought of how unbearable it would be for Maya to hate Frank for lying to Joan while she was lying to Cole.

'You always do this,' Maya said.

'Do what?'

'Make me believe we're making some kind of deal, and then break the deal I can't actually prove we made.'

Maya had everything to lose. The fact that she couldn't lose it drove her insane.

'Are you going to leave Cole?'

'Why would I do that? How would I do that...'

'I don't know.'

Lois and the Historian had never discussed what life, if any, there might be for them. Existing partners, children begotten and children lost had not come into it. They made no plans for a future together, instead snatching handfuls of time where they could, guzzling the hours down, like drinking liquor to stave off thirst. At home, they both continued to build their chronicle. His seemed richer, because of the children. Somewhere, the fact that he seemed to have more to lose than Lois became part of the justification.

'How much do you think they actually like this dog?' asked Lois.

'Dad pays more attention to the dog than to his grand-children,' said Maya.

'I'm thinking of stealing him.'

Lois decided not to tell Maya about Frank. Joan could tell

her herself, if she wanted to. Joan was a big girl. So was Maya. They were all adults. They were all entitled to ruin their lives, and to love.

6. Apron

THE LIGHTS FROM the other bank dotted the lake with milky sequins that moved with the wind. The sky was hiding its depth behind a lustre borrowed from the surface. Between lake and sky lay the mountains, like a black ribbon.

There were twice as many houses today as there were when they were growing up. The area where they lived was a strip of land between the forest and the water, a route from one end of the lake to the other. Most people just passed through on their way to town or to a higher altitude. It had changed a lot since they were kids. Now there was an organic bakery that showed classic films on Friday nights, an independent bookstore, a green market – comforts that Joan used as excuses for her tethering.

The noise from the main road came in through the kitchen window, which was cracked open. Lois watched her sister walk into the kitchen. She tried to imagine her transfixed and sloppy from love, but butted up against other, acquired visions. Maya was such a planner. She never ran out of anything. She always had spare toothbrushes for last-minute guests, extra bars of soap, glue sticks for the glue gun, white undershirts still in their packaging. Maya could usually see shit coming.

Simon walked over to the window and pressed his muzzle against the glass. As Lois slid the door open, the icy air sharpened her eyes. In the distance she saw her old senior school, which she recognised from the floodlit football pitch where she'd continued running on a broken toe to impress a boy. Next to the pitch was the bike shed where she'd picked up and quit smoking in Year Nine.

Simon walked out into the wintry night. Lois closed the door behind him. In the kitchen, Maya lit the stove and put the kettle on.

'Did you put Mum's apron on to make tea?' Lois asked.

'No. I was going to make a cake.'

'It's eleven o'clock. Why on earth would you make a cake now? There's cake everywhere already.'

'I'm feeling restless.'

'Absence makes the heart grow frantic.' She'd read that on a fortune cookie once. Maya remembered the breathing exercise. She lay down on the kitchen floor, in a spot where the underfloor heating had been historically reliable. Sharing the existence of Liz with Lois had given more weight to Liz's absence, suddenly put her missing on display. She wanted to tell Lois about the things they said to one another, about how dull her own precious children sometimes seemed when Liz hadn't given news for a while. She wanted Lois to know that she was more than just a wife – she was adored by a person who was better and smarter and more successful than either of them.

In the kitchen, Lois poured out two sherries.

'You're judging me,' said Maya. 'That's why you've stopped talking.'

'I'm definitely not doing that.'

'For years it's been French cartoons on YouTube so they grow up bilingual, and visualising how much space there is in the freezer, and having a box – I mean, a dedicated box – where I keep party favours for future birthdays, and now I'm listening to music again. I mean, like a teenager listening to music. You know? Where you think the songs are about you. It's tragic.'

Outside, Simon barked.

'She gets me books,' said Maya. 'Poetry books.'

'Oh no. Don't get into poetry, that's my thing.'

'Your thing… Do you know how tired I am of Mum calling me up to talk about you?'

'She does?'

'All the fucking time. Lois is having a hard time, I'm worried about Lois, Lois stopped seeing her therapist it's-such-a-shame-I-think-it-was-doing-her-good. Do you think Lois and Nick are trying again... Blah blah blah.'

Lois fetched the box of candied chestnuts from the pantry. 'Do you think we can eat these?'

'I don't fucking know,' said Maya.

'Will you eat one too, so if we weren't meant to, I can say it was your fault, and not be completely lying?'

Lois opened the box. She placed one of the chestnuts in its crinkly brown wrapper on her sister's chest. The chestnut went up and down with Maya's missing heart.

You never forget your first magic trick. When Lois was five, Frank made a chestnut appear from behind her ear. He made it disappear again behind her other ear. He tried and tried to conjure up the chestnut again, but couldn't. Lois asked her dad where the chestnut went, and Frank said it must have got lost inside her ear canal and travelled into her head. Frank seldom backed down from anything, least of all a joke. For years, Lois believed she had a chestnut lodged inside her cranium. In later years, when the missing chestnut was ruled a fiction, Lois kept a chestnut-shaped space inside her brain, a black hole on which she blamed all the missteps and regrettable turns of her teens, twenties and thirties.

Outside, Simon started barking again.

'He's going to wake up the children,' said Maya.

'I'll let him in.'

'I don't get that dog.'

'Why should he be get-able?'

'Why do you even say things like that?'

The front door opened, and Simon came bounding into the kitchen, followed by William.

He was carrying Frank's red rucksack – the one that had once transported Frank's past, present and future to this jagged part of the world. He was the spitting image of a young Frank – tall, kind-gloomy eyes and hair that seemed thicker than necessary.

'Fuck,' said Lois. 'I totally forgot. I'm so sorry.'

'It's OK,' said Wim, dropping the bag to the ground. 'I hitched a ride.'

'No one hitch-hikes any more,' said Maya.

'I do.'

Maya blew her brother a kiss from the ground.

'What's wrong with her?' he asked.

Lois shrugged and gave him a long, hard hug.

'Why didn't you call?' she asked.

'My phone was dead.'

Wim walked to the kitchen and opened the fridge. The order within was intimidating, so he shut the door and went looking for the reliable hard end of a baguette.

'Are you hungry?' asked Lois, handing him the box of chestnuts.

He took the box from her and unwrapped a chestnut.

'Where is everyone?' he asked.

'They're sleeping,' said Maya, extending a hand to be lifted up off the warm floor.

As William pulled Maya upright, Lois went to fetch the mystery Calvados from the dresser. The mystery Calvados had no label, and no one knew for sure where it came from. Frank said it had been given to him by a contractor. Joan insisted it was a present from Frank's late uncle in Normandy. The mystery Calvados was contained in a huge brown-glass jug, and had never been opened. It had been with them for as long as any of the kids could remember.

Lois uncorked the jug and poured some of the mystery Calvados into three fat little glasses etched with vines.

'I can't,' said Maya.

Lois rolled her eyes at her and raised her glass.

'This is a toast to our baby brother, who has deigned to join us at last. The last piece of the puzzle. We forgot you were coming, but we've been looking forward to seeing you. And just because you're an uncle, doesn't mean you're not a little shit. We both love you more than the others do, and more than we love the others. Welcome to the madhouse.'

The three of them clinked glasses. They were together for Christmas for the first time in five years. The last time they'd been together, Wim was still a boy. Not any more. Now he was in his last year at university, where he was learning how to prospect for ethereal values. It was the eve of all eves. A milestone or a notch, depending on your perspective.

'See you on the other side,' said Maya, downing her
Calvados.

*

Up in Lois's old bedroom, Gitsy's golden head was giving Joan
a cramp. Joan wriggled the girl out of her arms and hiked her
own head up the pillow. Finn's breathing was loud through
his sniffling cold, and Joan remembered how her own babies
had rattled in their cots, and how she had only half slept, in
order to keep an eye on them.

She wondered if Lois would ever have a child – a child
that looked like both of them. She longed to tell her she'd be
a good mother. But then again, she wasn't sure. There were
parts of Lois that seemed antithetical to devotion: the parts
that liked to lose it, disappear, or go on hiatus. As a teenager,
Lois sobbed frequently. Joan would find her in her room, eyes
red and cheeks shiny with tears. 'Why are you crying?' Joan
would ask. 'I don't know,' said Lois. And she didn't.

She worried about Lois, about how calm she was with
unhappiness, about how put-on her ferocity could seem.
With Maya she could be irrationally worried – like a parent
who worries their child is in the path of a cyclone, or stresses
about all the things that could go wrong with their health.
Cole and Maya were a front that took care of all the mundane
worries like money, health insurance, room to house guests…
When things got stressful at work they rented an old mill in

Virginia to decompress. Lois and Nick, on the other hand, seemed to be pursuing independent agendas with a common lack of vision.

She remembered how Lois had behaved on Nick's first visit – energetic and madcap, but also jealously guarding him, as though the family might steal him away from her.

It was an odd thing, she thought, to look more like one daughter but to feel more akin to the other. There were only two years separating Lois and Maya, and what they'd each done with time and age was completely different. Maya had fulfilled expectations at the first opportunity, and then gone and improved on them. And then there were the children. Their birth forged an unspoken and permanent understanding between Maya and Joan.

When Lois miscarried at three and a half months, Joan flew out to New York to stay with her for two weeks. She cleaned the apartment top to bottom and filled the fridge. Replaced the depleted shampoo bottles with fat white shampoo bottles from Khiel's, and got Lois a hot-water bottle. Threw out Nick's college flannel sheets and bought them the heavy, white bed linens of grown-ups. And while Lois was grateful, her mother's motherly efficiency had ultimately reinforced her own sense of uselessness.

These days, Joan was worried that Lois was wasting her talent. If she had committed to something, like Maya, she could have soared. She imagined Lois editing art books; big fat ones in hardback that she'd leave on the coffee table for her girlfriends to marvel at. Instead, Lois was a freelance translator, with no savings account and no commitment to a career. She took months out to go on poetry-writing residencies to work on a chapbook that got photocopied 150 times somewhere in the Midwest. She sent links to poems published online and PayPal requests for money to help pay for flights home.

Before going to sleep, Gitsy had asked Joan to read her a book she once read to Maya. Joan had read *Maisie Middleton*, and how she jumped up and down on her lazy parents' bed, clamouring for toast and jam. She made a note to send Frank out for eggs in the morning so she could make French toast for the kids.

'Now a memory story.'

'Hmm, let me think.'

'One that happened in real life.'

'A story with your mummy and auntie?'

'No, a story of you, when you were a little girl,' said Gitsy.

'How about a story that starts when I was a little girl, but also has a bit about your mummy and Auntie Lois?'

Joan's mother worked at a cigarette factory in the north of England. Her dad was a low-level manager at a stationery factory. For her sixth birthday, Joan had asked her mother for a pinafore she'd seen in a magazine. The pinafore was dark pink, made from crushed velvet, with lace trim and white ribbon ties. It was fancy – like a French maid's apron.

On the morning of her birthday, her parents presented her with a single parcel. In it was a perfect replica of the pinafore. In the front pocket, her father had slipped a notebook clasped shut by an elastic band that held a tiny black and white fountain pen.

For most of her adult life, Joan had tried to recreate this memory, or rather, the feeling of the memory – the way the ersatz apron had absorbed the world and spat it out perfect for a while. Her mother had perhaps made the apron one night, tired after a day packing cigarettes, and her father had probably found the notebook at work. But for some reason, the gift had answered a question unknown, filled a need so subconscious that Joan had felt her heart fall into place that day.

It was Lois who understood this, at the age of six, when she came into the living room, turned the volume all the way down on her mother's Frankie Goes to Hollywood record, and presented Joan with a package.

'Happy birthday, Mum.'

It wasn't her birthday.

'Thank you, darling. What is this?'

It was something that matched perfectly the shape that was now missing from the curtain in the tiny bedroom shared by Lois and Maya. It was a little pink apron, with white shoelaces for ties and white-out lace on the border. Sellotaped to the front was a pocket – another chunk from the curtains – containing a notebook, bound with more sellotape, with a pen sellotaped to it.

'With each copy,' said Joan, 'the apron became more special.'

But Gitsy was fast asleep. Looking at the curtains, Joan thought it was probably for the best Gitsy had missed the last part. The curtains had been a gift for Maya, when they moved into the new house. They were log-cabin, in blues and pinks – Maya's favourite colours back then.

Joan turned off the bedside lamp and walked over to her room. Tonight Frank had fallen asleep in bed instead of in front of the news. The kids must have kicked him out of the living room. Joan liked the idea of the children disturbing Frank's routine. It could only be good for him. Frank's presence in the bed reversed their natural order. She hadn't climbed into a bed that contained Frank in a long time, although he usually materialised by sunrise.

At first, him sliding into bed at two or three in the morning used to wake her up. But after a while she learned to sleep through his later boarding – learned to sleep through Frank. She thought she heard William's voice downstairs, and wondered whether the children would remember to let the dog out for a pee before bedtime. And if they did, whether they would remember to let him back in afterwards.

She considered waking Frank up, telling him she knew

about Heide. She thought of humiliating him by pointing out how much she knew about his innermost thoughts. What a strange idea: humiliating someone with evidence of their capacity to love. She wondered how Frank would react. Probably he wouldn't. She thought of how taxing that lack of reaction would be on her. It would all be her burden to shoulder. Just like Christmas. Just like just about everything.

She must love Frank like a mother, because that was the only brand of love whose instinct was to shrug in the face of sabotage. What would happen to all that motherly, wifely love when she left him?

If she left him.

Maybe she could settle the matter with a letter. But the idea of Frank responding with his own, self-exonerating letter was too exhausting even to think of. She looked at Frank's shape in the bed. His mouth was open and his head tilted back. He looked quite dead.

Would it make her happy to leave him? Would she feel freer if she lived alone? It occurred to her for the first time that, while she wouldn't be leaving him for his bad habits, a separation would take care of those, too. No more beard residue in the bathroom sink. No cutting bread directly on the table. It would be like a bonus.

She would miss the day trips to Turin, she thought, when she left him. she left him. They still did that, every now and again – drove to Turin for a meal and a mosey around an

Italian supermarket. Or did they? On the other hand, she wouldn't need to get used to the idea of going to bed alone. She considered whether this was just another decision that would be delicately forced on her, like studying languages instead of art at university. Decisions like that had a way of making you believe they were for the best.

Downstairs, Lois was making one of her loud, drunken toasts. She'd leave them to it. She could wait one more night to see them all together. As she slid in bed next to Frank and his pitiful old-man secret, Joan tried to be sad, but only managed to feel lucky.

*

Like millions of his peers before him, Frank had let himself be swayed by the promise of instant conversation and life-altering reconnection. He had been presented with abstracts of the various social media platforms by his three children, who not only contradicted each other, but also hierarchised the platforms according to different criteria. It concerned him that his offspring, who spanned barely more than a decade, couldn't agree on what it meant to 'be active', and where one should concentrate said activity. He was older than any of them by at least thirty-five years, so where did that leave him?

Like others before him, Frank looked out of a window at a familiar landscape, and hoped the world would give up a suitable alias. When this didn't happen, he thought about it for the next forty-eight hours, writing the various possibilities out on a piece of paper to see how they read. Once he settled on a pseudonym (greenlit by Wim), he spent the next three weeks being conspicuously inactive.

And then one day, the thought of Heide came to him like a bat out of hell. Later he decided the memory had been dredged up under duress, after having the promise of 'reconnection' rammed down his throat one too many times.

It took no time for Frank's latent curiosity about H to blow up into a round-the-clock obsession. First he found out that she owned an art gallery in Hamburg. Then he found out that she frequented other people's art openings, also in Hamburg. Finally, he found her. There she was, in a long black coat, towering black heels and dark-red lipstick. The only thing in the way of their reconnection was a friendship request. And so Frank requested her friendship – a gesture that seemed superficial, given that they'd once lived together for several golden months, and slept on top of each other in Frank's metal twin bed. The fear of having made a fool of himself and the fear of having to stare at his (so far) unrequited friendship request were such that Frank had to walk away from his laptop for two days.

When he returned, she had accepted. As easily as she had turned him down back in 1975, she had taken him back into her fold.

While their renewed friendship remained a thing

unconsummated, Frank travelled back and forth between the present and the memory of his stillborn relationship with Heide. He made the journey so frequently in the week after H accepted his request that by day seven he jumped straight from 2014 to 1975, eluding the decades gone by.

Frank wanted to crawl inside Heide's brain and see what was left of him there. In thoughts he invoked her name three times – Heide Heide Heide – until he started saying it out loud, in the street, while walking the dog.

Then came the missive. 'Well…?' she asked. By that point, Frank knew the rudiments of social media navigation. He knew she had no children, no husband, and nothing more than a feeble, irregular attachment to a curator called Klaus who didn't even live in Hamburg.

'Your email address?' he replied, as though social media, having completed its goal, were now obsolete. Like any other disposable article you use once and then toss. Half an hour after this exchange, at the small corner table in the backroom of Chez Josée, some heart was consumed.

Frank pretended to be asleep as Joan got into bed. She stayed on her side of the middle dip (the mattresses were twins joined together by a king-size sheet with elasticated corners, and could always be separated). Lying in the dark, Frank constructed a new letter to H in his head. H had become one of his permanent concerns. He imagined it was H lying next to him, not Joan. Unlike Joan, who turned one year older every year, H appeared in his mind as a twenty-four-year-old. After his initial detective work, he never looked for pictures of her online. Frank closed his eyes, and the image of H melted momentarily under a stronger vision of vegetables and an egg, captured in shimmering aspic. It was sometimes a starter at Chez Josée. He opened his eyes again to lose the food, and beckon once more the face of H.

There she was, asleep on the bed, her toes curled like a ballerina's. One of her legs was resting on the other, dropping a light-grey shadow on the skin of her calf. The back of her knee was a warm, dark fold. He remembered her thighs – or did he? He thought maybe he had spent some time there, prized between her thighs, like a toddler a mother keeps near during a picnic on a cliff. And then her ass, and her back, arched in sleep, and up to her shoulders, dotted with freckles... Freckles? Frank, who was on his way to sleep, rolled closer to the woman. Joan's breath reached him gently, waking the skin on his face.

He thought of all the things Joan had done for him – body and soul. Chopping, raking, waiting, birthing, ironing, settling, counting, decorating, driving, hiking. He was one of her beneficiaries, one of the people she gave to, again and again, perhaps as an excuse not to address her own needs.

*

Last night you were in my dream. You had a spattered apron

and a blue shirt rolled up at the sleeves. You had come to the house to help us cook Christmas dinner. You took breaks like a worker, and smoked cigarettes.

I'd like to lick your ears. I'd like you not to wipe off the drool.

Last night I dreamed we'd gone to Corsica for Christmas. Mum and Dad had rented a house. We've never been to Corsica.

I forgot.

Me and you saw a big rainbow and we saw a motorcycle. It was a snow day. There were many snow days and we went home, took a nap, then played, then took a nap, and we had lunch, dinner and breakfast cereal and we went to bed.

I dreamed I had decided to repair one of the old wooden docks on the lake. Once, I rode my bicycle off one of those docks. It fell on me and my ankle got stuck in the spokes. I could see the sky through the water, and it looked wobbly. In the dream I was using cement, and I was working underwater, and when I said I needed a trowel, you went to the village to buy me one.

You were exceptionally nice to me in this dream. Nice like thoughtful.

You tied my cock with kitchen twine. You tied it so hard I was afraid it would break off.

You showed me your orchard and the trees your great-grandfather planted. You showed me the birdhouse you made when you were ten. You showed me a cupboard of stacked quilts and soft towels. You have a dryer in the mudroom. You have an actual fucking mudroom.

You blink too much.

We smoked and drank beer, and I told you my husband doesn't drink beer, wouldn't know how to order a beer. You didn't find him foolish because of this. The house spun round and round but we couldn't feel it because of all the padding from the quilts.

I want to shower with you.

I want to shower you with acts of kindness.

Can you overuse artificial tears? I mean, could you drown in them?

I dream that I'm leaning over an abyss, and everyone is laughing at me. I'm holding onto a tree so I don't fall. I'm getting vertigo and the drop is going to my head. You're down there, in the abyss. Everyone I love is either laughing at me or down there in the abyss. I want to wake up but when I do, I'm still dreaming.

I told you I was a gender expert. You said, yes, I know, it says so on your apron.

I never dream.

I have a whole chapter about your town. About it being a centre of the French Resistance.

Yes, do it like in the dream.

Watch out for the holes in the dream.

147

We really need a map to this dream.
Come close to me, it feels soft.
We are all volunteers.
Good houses always have cold bathrooms.
I think ich liebe dich.
This dream is going to my head.
This dream is going straight to my head.

7. Oysters

AND THEN IT was Christmas Eve. A sacred day, divided into two, the first ten hours spent preparing a celebration that would last perhaps five. Later, sleep would come – a lull between rituals that had gained layers with the years, and aged slower than the children.

As the crumbs of brown sugar became molten between the bread and the skillet that was only ever used for pancakes or French toast, Joan looked at her three adult babies, sitting in their respective spots at the breakfast table. Lois and Maya seemed gigantic on the bench where they'd once bickered and concealed their greens under the edge of their plates. Squeezed between them was Gitsy, in longjohns and snow boots. Finn was on his mother's lap, stretching his little hand out towards the butter knife. William sat at the end of the table, in the spot where he'd once gurgled and spun the built-in beads on his high chair. The high chair was still around in the basement somewhere, but Finn turned his nose up at it, tensing his little body and screaming at the top of his lungs every time he was introduced to it. Nick and Cole sat in the parents' chairs, no longer occupied by the parents – who were retired from the job of refereeing family meals.

The predictable absence of Frank from the breakfast table was matched by an enigmatic absence of weather outside, as though a bubble had trapped a stagnant second of December and kept the air perfectly still around the lake. Frank and Joan noted this at exactly the same time – Joan from the kitchen, and Frank from his office.

The French toast was seared but still bouncy enough for Joan's back-of-the-fork test – the first rite of a day that would deliver dozens more.

'We were going to do no gifts this year, but instead we thought we'd do cheap, tacky gifts,' said Lois.

'Isn't that what you did last year?' said Maya.

Wim laughed at his reliable, hungover sisters. Maya had woken up with a stinking headache from her three and a half drinks, for which she blamed Lois. Finn had been up since five. He had spent the first twenty minutes of the day loudly rejecting the bottle of formula. When he finally gave in and guzzled down the bottle, he looked up at her with big, quizzical eyes, and Maya felt guilty. She'd forgotten to swear

Lois to secrecy about Liz, but she also knew the only person Lois might tell was Nick, and she could live with that.

'Where's Dad?' asked Wim.

'In a parallel universe,' said Lois.

Joan put the French toast on the table, and went to beat the eggs for her ten-egg dried-fig brioche.

Joan wondered whether Lois had told Maya and William about Frank. She had told Lois for no other reason than that Lois was the daughter that looked the most like her. Telling Lois felt a bit like going back in time and warning her younger self. Lois hadn't mentioned anything since their phone conversation last week. She wondered if the children saw her as long-suffering. The thought sent a shiver down her spine. She was pretty sure none of them saw Frank as long-suffering.

'This is why I come home all the time,' said Wim. 'Mum's famous French toast.'

'What do you mean, famous?' said Lois. 'You say it like it's a Mum thing.'

'It is a Mum thing.'

'Mum's made French toast maybe three times in her life.'

'What are you talking about? She used to make it all the time.'

Joan listened to the children argue over the Truth. Perhaps one day, after she and Frank were dead, the children would sit down for breakfast and Lois would recall how Frank had become a socialised hermit in his sixties. Perhaps Wim would remember things differently. Perhaps Maya would say, rubbish, he was always that way. Joan decided to keep the Truth about the frequency of the French toast to herself, even if they asked. They didn't ask.

'Can someone pick up the oysters?' Joan asked the husbands, thinking they might like to come up for air.

'I'll go,' Nick volunteered.

'I'll go with you,' said Cole.

'They have a lobster tank,' Nick told Gitsy. 'If you come with us, you might get to pet a lobster.'

'I wanna go!' screamed Gitsy. She kicked off the snow boots and ran upstairs to get dressed.

In his office Frank heard Gitsy, and remembered a game the girls used to play while sledding. They would start screaming at the top of the hill and keep screaming for as long as they could, or until the sled came to a stop. Whichever came first. He wondered how long he had left before he was made to pitch in with the Christmas chores.

Today would be a long, introverted kind of day, strung together from last-minute errands and contributions, a crucial kind of day that would be eclipsed by its last waking hours – hours they all knew had to become memorable. Christmas 2015: it had the potential either to resemble itself, descend into chaos, or both. The same thing that had happened every year for seventeen years would today happen differently, as it did every Christmas Eve.

Tonight's party would have several concentric rings of celebration. Gitsy would be up for the first, and would spend most of it negotiating access to the second. With a bit of luck, Finn would be banned from Christmas Eve altogether and put to bed early. The second circle would involve a toast, and the passing around of thinly sliced things topped with fish roe. Frank would oversee the third stage, with its two round trays of oysters and dishes of vinegar sauce that would gravitate around the table like sacraments. The family would murder oysters until ten-ish, when Frank would be forced by the others to sing a song by the Dubliners in his terrible French accent. Frank would stay up until the fourth circle of Christmas Eve, which ended after Joan's foie gras. *This year* he would pretext exhaustion, but spend another two or three hours in the office, writing to H or expounding some aspect of German Romanticism for his blog-tome. Joan would give up at circle five, after the dainty china cups came out for coffee, and kiss her children goodnight. She would go upstairs, change into her nightgown and bathrobe, and come back down with bags of presents that had been wrapped exquisitely days ago, by someone not in a rush. Cole would try to get Maya to bed in circle six, but *this year* Maya would be texting well into circle eight, which involved drinking games and poor decisions by Wim and Lois. Nine would be the Kate Bush karaoke dance party in the basement, with whisky, or perhaps *this year* more mystery Calvados. Level-eight-drunk

Lois would be too much for Nick, who would by then have given up on sex and gone to bed alone.

But all that was yet to come, or perhaps it wasn't at all. Perhaps Lois and Nick would go to bed at the same time and fuck each other's brains out while Santa tiptoed around in the dark in her slippers. Perhaps Frank would turn his computer off before dinner and put it away in his briefcase, on its special shelf. Perhaps this would be the year Cole got blind drunk, and interrupted one of Frank's scholarly anecdotes with a nicely soused ohfuckoff. Perhaps Gitsy would fall asleep without a fight in front of *The Muppets' Christmas Carol*, and perhaps *this year* Joan would announce she didn't believe in shooting puréed food down a duck's gullet until its liver tripled in size.

*

After breakfast, Wim walked over to Tara's house with a tin Joan had filled with mince pies. 'Give Tara's mum my compliments on her wreath,' said Joan. Relations between the two families had broken down in May, when Tara's parents added their names to the neighbourhood petition against the eastward spread of Frank's bamboos.

As he crossed the curtain of bamboos that separated Frank's gullied no-man's-landscape from next door's hygienic lawn and weedless beds, William saw his girlfriend's back through the window of her bedroom. She appeared to be looking down at her phone. She jumped when he rapped at the window.

Wim couldn't remember the last time he'd used the front door. It probably predated his voice breaking. As kids, they went in and out of each other's houses without knocking. Tara's family moved into the house next door when Wim was still in middle school. Back when the neighbourhood kids attached fake speedometers to their handlebars, and pegged playing cards to their spokes. They would cycle around the neighbourhood for hours on end on their pretend motorcycles, riding them down the gentle stream that cut their street in two. Sometimes they cycled all the way down to the lake, off the canoe dock and into the water. They bummed roll-ups from Tara's older brother and smoked them in the tall grass field behind the bakery. In the summer, they spied through the hedges on the stunning blonde who sunbathed topless by her pool. Rumour was she'd been on television in the eighties and had a twenty-year-old boyfriend. If she left for the weekend, they annexed the pool at night, adding their cigarette butts to her overflowing ashtray. In late September they had rotten-apple fights in the trees.

Wim climbed through the window and put the mince pies down on the desk. He kissed Tara on the mouth for a long time. The bedroom had that familiar smell of patchouli incense that also infused all of Tara's clothing, books, hair and skin. The smell was strongest in the crook of her neck.

'Hi,' he said.

She kissed him again, and they moved to the bed. Tara ran

her fingers through Wim's too-long, messy hair. 'When did you last get a haircut?' she asked, taking her shirt off. Wim thought it would be nice to take a nap, save the Talk for later.

In the second year of senior school, Tara started hanging out with the theatre crowd, which put their friendship on a two-year hiatus. They still saw each other around all the time. At the bus stop. At school. On the beach. The canoe dock. At the bowling alley on a Friday or Saturday night. Then Tara got a boyfriend – a kid who worked as a ski instructor in the winter and a kiteboard instructor in the summer. She lost her virginity to him, and it lasted through two seasons. Wim did not have a girlfriend in high school, although he could have gone out with a girl called Sophie had he wanted to. Somehow the realistic option of a senior-school girlfriend proved satisfying enough for him, on top of which he was spared the need to engage in humiliating displays of frenching in corridors during break.

And then, before they knew it, senior school was over.

The night before he left for London to study economics, Wim bumped into Tara in the old town, in a bar frequented for its two-euro tequila sunrises. She was there with her theatre posse, a purple cocktail umbrella behind her ear. She gave him hell about his choice of degree, and asked why he wasn't going to art school like her. Or film school. Anything but economics. She brought up the cloud-tank video. 'Is it because of your parents?' she asked. 'Despite them,' he answered.

Later, they walked home together along the cycle path, stopping at the marina for the summer's swansong swim. The water was warm, and the sand beneath their feet shone silver in the moonlight. The mountain across the lake was yellow and cratered. At its feet was the other bank, its magnificence on hold until sun-up.

After the swim they dried off with their clothes, and Wim lent Tara Frank's Albertville 1992 T-shirt. As they lay on the dock, gazing up at the stars, he noticed the Olympic flame go up and down with the heaving of her chest. The thought of Tara's breasts and heart under the fabric of his shirt was a revelation. Over the years, he and Tara had skinny-dipped in the neighbour's pool, shared a tent, spent hours together at the beach, and yet, somehow, he'd completely missed the fact that she had a body. Tara caught him staring at her and giggled.

They walked home the short way, cutting through the field at the back of the supermarket. When they got to the car park Tara grabbed Wim's hand and pulled him close. For almost an hour they made out against the shopping-trolley shed, stopping every now and again to say nothing. The next day, Wim left for London. They didn't see each other again until the following summer, when Tara's plan to go backpacking through Italy fell through because her girlfriend came down with appendicitis.

At first they met at the municipal beach. She moved her towel close to his. Then it was shows, a movie, a music festival. Hiking and smoking weed in the mountain behind their houses. By the middle of the summer they were spending each day together, stocking up on their reserves of one another for September, when Wim would return to London and Tara to art school in Lyon.

Commitment excited them. It wasn't something you were meant to take on at their age – the precociousness felt reckless. The relationship was something they shared, something that set them apart from their peers, but it was also this thing they got to take back to university with them, individually, like a habit.

They used every tool their generation had to offer to manage the distance. Had long text conversations about what would happen next, when Tara was an artist, and Wim understood the economy. Wim wanted Tara to join him in London, where he'd find a job in the City. She thought she might, but also, perhaps they could both go to Berlin instead, and live in a squat. In a flat, said Wim.

William was the sensible one, but in a sense he was also the most artful, if not artistic, because his chosen career path required feats of imagination that even Tara couldn't begin to comprehend. Wim planned one day to own a huge house with a studio for Tara. A small sailing boat with walnut berths. A holiday home in the part of Sicily his great-grandmother came from.

'I want to tell you something,' he said.

'No you don't.'

Tara climbed off him and sat on the edge of her bed. She looked beautiful, unflawed, not like his sisters, who were women who had grown up and become less attractive, but more interesting. Wim sat up and kissed her again. Breathed her in once more.

'If you wanted to tell me something, you'd just tell me,' she said, putting her shirt back on. 'This preamble means you're either scared to tell me or you don't know how to.'

The first crack had been during reading week. He was due to come back to France to spend the week with Tara in Lyon. He ran out of money for an airfare, and instead drove to Whitby with his room-mate and his room-mate's friends. One of the friends was Ruth. When it became obvious to him that if he continued talking to Ruth, they'd continue to find common ground and edge closer to each other until something happened, he stopped seeing as much of Ruth, but resolved to break up with Tara so he could see more of Ruth.

Tara had watched him grow into a man across a divisive bamboo hedge. Had watched him navigate adolescence and senior school, which was like watching someone almost bleed to death but then make it. Their attraction was complicated by the past. Any future together could only ever be a continuation of their shared childhood. The point was, she reminded him too much of him.

With Ruth, he had to start from the beginning. At first it felt childish to compare favourite bands and films with a girl. Childish but imperative. He and Tara had skipped that stage, where lust is built on common ground and texting songs is foreplay. They already knew those things about each other, and in time revised their childhood friendship as one long flirtation.

It wasn't that he didn't love Tara – it was more that their love was a project. It was possible he would end up with Tara one day, and it was possible he wouldn't. She was everything that was familiar, and she was a far-fetched possibility. Besides, the two-year break-up was more or less written into their history. Once, Lois told him it was unlikely he'd grow old with a girl he'd once pelted with brown, rotting apples. Unlikely he'd marry the girl with whom he smoked cigarettes without inhaling.

He tried to bring his head closer to Tara's face to inhale her reassuring patchouli essence.

'Are you seeing someone else?' she asked.

'No,' said Wim.

'But you would like to. If the opportunity presents itself.'

Wim thought he must be stupid to let such an intelligent woman go. It reminded him of fishing with Frank, of how they would sometimes catch and release. You released the fish, not because it wasn't perfect, not because it wouldn't feed you, but because it happened to be the first one you'd caught. At the end of the day you'd take home whatever fish bit, but while the day was still young, it was just sport.

'I knew it,' she said.

She didn't give him enough credit. She was acting as if he was a disappointment. He'd gone for months without thinking this. For months he'd been deeply committed to their relationship, giving other girls the cold shoulder and responding to all of Tara's texts – even when he was out at night. This wasn't the culmination of months of shitty behaviour away from her. There had been no lies. This was a recent, responsible decision.

He thought of that night, a couple of weeks ago, at a nightclub called the Coliseum. It was a nineties night, which was too far back to mean anything, but not ancient enough to merit an entire night. Ruth was at the club with some friends. She had on tights that were laddered, and wore black nylon stockings as a top over a black bra. He watched her make out with someone up against a mock-Grecian column. On the bus home he texted Tara that he loved her. He didn't know what it meant to be thinking of that now.

He wondered if Tara had met someone else. She was smart, gorgeous in a way that defied statistics. He didn't ask. Instead, he opened the tin of mince pies Joan had packed.

'I always thought we'd be the ones to make it,' said Tara.

'Me too.'

'But also I didn't.'

'Yeah.'

The mince pies released their reliable Christmas taste, which mixed in with the sweetness already in the room. Wim felt like an adult. He had done something even his parents couldn't pull off. He would go home to them now, and to his sisters, who were each following their chosen course, and for once the big change would be happening to him. It almost felt good to give up on the perfect woman, knowing full well you'd done nothing more than what the world had expected from you all along.

*

Capping a pyramid of ice chips, the oysters looked like a back-to-front mountain. Like a stony drift come to rest on a pile of snow – and not the other way round. At the foot of the oyster mountain, a garland of seaweed emanated the smell of brine from its shiny green blisters.

Cole pulled out a number from the ticket dispenser: 636. Their house number.

'What else do we need?' said Nick, pulling out Joan's shopping list, which had been scribbled on the back of a restaurant bill from Chez Josée. 'Milk, lemons, baking powder, toilet paper, FORMULA, clams.' He read aloud, trying to do justice to Maya's capitalisation.

'Does she say what kind of formula?' asked Cole.

'No.'

Cole hoped there were only three kinds of French formula, and only one of them organic.

'How do you say tin of clams in French?' asked Nick.

'Clementine,' said Gitsy, rocking the shopping trolley to and fro.

The number 631 appeared on the red LED display behind the fish counter. A woman stepped forward and ordered some cooked prawns.

'Gitsy, why don't you run over there and get the lemons,' said Cole, pointing to the fruit section. Gitsy skipped off.

'They have clams right here,' said Cole.

'Oh no. They have to be the shitty kind in a tin. For clam dip. It's this thing my parents always make at Christmas.'

Nick thought of his parents, and how it would be just the two of them tonight, eating clam dip and listening to Christmas jazz albums. He'd taken Lois home one year. But his parents' Christmas routine was so well honed at this point that it allowed parallel experience, but not inclusion.

'What's Christmas like at your parents'?' Nick asked Cole.

'Oh, just like here, but without any of the French stuff.'

Nick marvelled at how well Cole seemed to have found his place in this family. His effect on the family was one of simplification. Grandparenting was easier with him around. He spoke French effortlessly, thus simplifying mealtimes with Frank. He took care of his wife in the way parents dream their daughters be taken care of.

Nick, on the other hand, was a man post-humiliation. Expected to hurry up and feel once again the legitimacy of being the man Lois had chosen to bring into this fold. He wanted them all to understand that if anyone was on probation right now, it was her. Back home at his parents' house, his baby stocking still hung from the fireplace – proof that he too was the centre of a world.

Gitsy returned with a bag bulging with lemons.

'That's far too many lemons, darling,' said Cole.

She tried to swing the bag over the side of the shopping trolley but lost her grip, and the lemons fell to the floor, rolling away from the trolley in all directions.

The number 633 flashed on the display screen.

Cole and Nick chased the scattered lemons, crouching down to pick them up, under the gaze of French people who seemed not in the habit of dropping lemons like tourists.

Number 633 ordered a thick slab of pink seafood terrine and scallops on the half-shell. Cole wondered whether number 633 had been sent on an errand by his wife, and how many errands a typical week contained. How were tasks divided in his household? By which process did each chore fall on either side of the line? Or perhaps number 633 lived alone, and would spend Christmas Eve with friends. Maybe he would drive home through town later tonight, return to a solitude he either valued or bore.

Number 634 was a child barely older than Gitsy. The child

said something in French, and the fishmonger walked over to the lobster tank. Gisty followed the boy to the tank and watched the man pull four brown-spotted lobsters out of the water.

'What is he going to do with them?' she asked, turning to her father.

'Drop them in a big pot of boiling water,' said her uncle.

Gitsy looked at the boy, who circled the tank to receive a plastic bag of live lobsters, their impotent claws fastened with blue elastic bands.

'Can we do that?' she asked.

'No, we're having oysters,' said Nick.

'I don't actually like oysters,' said Cole. 'But I think I'm expected to participate anyway.'

A participator. That's exactly what he was.

Earlier, Nick wondered how often Cole and Maya had sex. If that part of their lives was just a continuation of the efficiency on display elsewhere. He was sure he'd seen Lois wince the other day. It was a passing look, but as it flashed across her face it left its mark there.

Number 635 in the line went unclaimed and the display changed to 636. Cole and Nick both took a step forward, and Gitsy walked hopefully back to the lobster tank.

'You go,' said Cole.

Nick asked for three dozen oysters. The oysters came in a wooden crate, packed in ice. Gitsy sat in the trolley next to them, holding the too-many lemons in her lap.

Cole hesitated in the formula aisle, picking up the boxes and scrutinising the labels. Watching his brother-in-law pick out feed for his son, Nick suddenly felt quite free. Like he hadn't fully anchored himself to these people yet. Like a floating island. An island in the middle of a pristine Alpine lake. An island that might just wake up one morning and decide to float away.

*

It took Finn forty-eight hours to nuzzle into the smell of his grandmother. At first he cried whenever Maya left the room, but now he was quite happy to play at Joan's feet, and to direct his big questioning silences at her. Happy to take a handful of her trousers in his little fist and pull himself up to her knees. Finn went to his grandmother like the dog went to her. Silently, and unsure of what it was he needed.

Cole and Gitsy were taking a nap upstairs. Lois and Nick were somewhere in the house, and Frank... Well, Frank. Maya kissed her baby on the head and bent down to strap the leash to the dog's collar.

'Oh, he'll be fine without that, darling,' said Joan.

'Well, I don't want him to run out in front of a car.'

'Why would he run out in front of a car? He's not stupid.'

Simon did not alter his expression to confirm this. The gormless face, he found, appeared to make the humans feel the most secure.

'You need anything, Mum?'

'Pick up some yogurts for the kids.'

'They don't eat them.'

'Pick up some yogurts for your father, then.'

'OK.'

Maya wrapped her mother's scarf around her neck and put on her mother's fur toque. She and Lois always helped themselves to their mother's clothes. She didn't mind, they thought.

Outside the sky was blue like an inkpot, and the mountain-tops were still fishing for the light that drained from the valley. As soon as she left the driveway, Maya took her phone out and dialled Liz.

'Hi. You've reached Liz. I can't get to the phone right now but leave me a mess—'

'She's at work,' Maya told Simon, but what she meant to say was, 'I love her more than she loves me.' She was shocked to realise she had just spoken to the dog.

Simon was taking a piss, and wishing Maya would slacken the leash. How could she not understand how unpleasant it was to have to feel the tautness of a leash while pissing?

Maya removed her glove to text Liz. She thought of Liz, spending Christmas in Turkey where she was leading a workshop on gender equality in the workplace. She wondered what kind of women would be attending the workshop.

Hey. I miss you. Pick up.

Simon shook his back leg and stepped into the road. The wet road scintillated in the orange street lights. The lights were ugly and efficient, and buzzed as if they were on a permanent timer. The first time Nick had visited their parents' house, he'd told the girls it reminded him of LA. Maya had scoffed, but years later, after a trip to LA, she knew exactly what he meant. Balconied hills and no two houses the same. Greenery everywhere and hidden driveways that snaked off to lush gardens – some of which had pools. Random fields for walking. A dictatorship of hills and monticules. Maya's phone buzzed.

Can't talk now. Later? Miss you too. So much.

Maya fumbled in the dark and dragged Simon to the next street light.

I feel like I'm in purgatory here. Without you.

Simon was looking at the field between the small back road up to Joan and Frank's house and the main road, which they'd have to cross to get to the supermarket. He tugged at the leash. The mud was frozen solid but the damp was releasing the smell of winter grass and soil, and as it mixed with the pitch-black, it became something Simon needed to experience. He pulled harder.

'Wait. Come here.'

Simon went to Maya, who undid his leash. He panted gratefully at her and ran into the field until she couldn't see him any more. Her phone vibrated.

Gotta go.

'Simon. Simon!' she yelled. 'Get back here!'

The road was silent except for the purr of cars in the distance.

Maya's chest tightened. She didn't have the energy to run after a dog. To go looking for a dog in the dark. She didn't have the energy to go home and tell her parents their precious dog was gone.

'Simon! Get back here you stupid dog!'

Something behind her made her jump. Simon was there, on the other side of the road, sniffing a road sign. He looked up at her, and Maya thought he looked different – almost human.

At the main road, cars were whizzing home on their way back from last-minute errands. There was no light, so they had to wait for a gap in the traffic to run to the island, and then wait again to get to the other side. The supermarket was a square steel compound with a neon-blue sign that flickered in every window of Frank's house. It was flanked by the Buffalo Bill Tex-Mex grill, and a now defunct nightclub. Maya remembered how, when she was growing up, the nightclub, with its velvet red-rope entrance and film-negative neon, had seemed to be the height of sophistication. She tied Simon to the post by the trolleys and walked inside the store.

The store was warm, and smelled like a French supermarket at Christmas – a mix of red meat and chocolate truffles. A pan-pipe Christmas mix played on loop over the PA system. She picked up a basket and headed over to the toiletries section, to the men's products. She took the cap off a bottle of aftershave and sniffed it. It smelled of juniper and of Cole. She thought of how Liz's smell was always the smell of something else. And how something else was always the smell of Cole. It had that good, serious French pharmaceutical packaging, and it looked more expensive than a supermarket gift, so she put it in the basket. Behind the cosmetics aisle was the underwear. She picked out a value pack of socks and another one of boxers. The boxers were tartan. She threw some nets of chocolate money into the basket for the kids, and went to the booze section. Cole didn't drink much, but she felt bad about giving him only underwear and aftershave. At the end of the aisle was a display with gigantic jars of cherries in brandy. The jar had a gold lid and a label that was meant to look handwritten. She put it in her basket and went to the till.

On a break. I can't believe I'm spending Christmas at a goddamn Sheraton.

Paying for her items, Maya wondered whether the Sheraton had a swimming pool. Outside, she untied Simon and they walked back up the hill.

Me and this other workshop leader asked the kitchen if they could make us turkey. We're going to have a mini-celebration on my balcony.

Maya thought of Liz in a fluffy white hotel bathrobe, eating turkey with her co-worker on the balcony of her bedroom. She knew she had no right to be jealous. She was the one going to sleep next to her husband each night, waking up in a mushy pile of plush toys and the children they'd made together.

Thank God she's here. I was feeling really lonely without you.

Maya flung the phone as far as she could into the field, which was by now as dark and as uninviting as a black hole. After a while she waded into the tall grass, and kept her ears peeled for the second buzz notification. If it came, she didn't hear it.

'Fetch!'

Simon looked at her from the road, little clouds of hot breath coming from his nostrils. Maya tried again.

'Fetch! Now.'

Simon started to walk up the hill, back towards the house.

'Wait!' cried Maya, jumping over the short ditch and catching up with him. The night at her back felt like too big a wave, just waiting to break.

*

Lois followed the draught down the stairs to the basement, where Frank's house continued to dig itself deeper into a hole. The house was separated from the basement – itself only partially sealed off from the elements – by a simple plywood door with a five-inch gap. You had an agonised-over underfloor heating pattern upstairs and a five-inch-gap that let in the cold downstairs.

Lois called for Simon, but he didn't appear. It occurred to her that she had only called out his name once before, during a storm. Simon usually showed up uninvited.

In the last room of the cellar, Frank had built up an alcove with what looked like summer-camp bunk beds. He'd drilled and screwed three dozen two-by-fours into a junction of slats and shelves, on two levels, to store the children's expanding archive. The shelves were buckling under the weight of boxes marked 'Lois', 'Maya' and 'Wim'. Being the youngest, William only had two boxes from senior school and a couple of boxes containing Lego and leftovers from his Egyptologist phase.

As a boy, Wim liked to pretend that the basement was the tomb of a pharaoh, and that those who entered would be cursed for all eternity. Believing himself cursed, and therefore immune to any further malediction, he led candlelit expeditions in and out of each room, passing off the family junk as ancient mortuary accessories. Joan once joked that Frank's expansions were consumed by Wim's basement excavations, and that only their two obsessions in tandem could guarantee the house's structural soundness.

Maya had purged most of her belongings or had them shipped, and her stuff took up only one of the bunks. But Lois had already relegated several lives to her parents' basement. There were accumulations from two failed relationships (one of which had been firmly on its way to a premature engagement), the legacy of existences in two countries, and a collection of books that was both unselective and unrealistic. Somewhere in there was also her whisky collection.

The collection hadn't been started by her, but by Greg, a former neighbour. After suffering a minor stroke in 2008, doctors told him to lay off the booze for good. He pushed a box containing fifteen bottles of whisky across the corridor to Lois's apartment one afternoon. There was a Bunnahabhain 25 Year Old, a thirty-year-old Isle of Jura, and a dozen or so more bottles. Three unopened, many of them half full, a few with only an inch of the stuff left. When she and her boyfriend had split up, and she'd moved to the US to pursue her Masters, Lois had given away her furniture to friends, but driven the bequeathed whisky back to her parents' house. It had been maturing in their basement for seven years.

Simon suddenly appeared in the room, and leaned his clumsy weight against her thigh.

'You don't know this, Simon, but in my family, I'm always the first to get drunk at Christmas. If I were ever to get pregnant, which I probably won't ever again, I could never be pregnant over Christmas. That would ruin it for everyone.'

A few days after the miscarriage, Lois had spent several hours in a local Irish bar, dominating the jukebox. There were four other people in the bar that night. She told them how she'd stood in Union Square for three hours with her prescription for Misoprostol, not wanting to go home to expel what was left inside her. As long as she was on the square, she said, as long as the prescription was unfulfilled, things didn't feel quite so final. Later in the evening she felt bad for oversharing, and bought everyone a round of top-shelf whisky. And then another. When she stumbled in around 2 a.m., Nick held her hair back as she retched into the toilet.

The shelves in the basement were four boxes deep, and it took a fair amount of box-Tetris for Lois to get her hands on the booze.

There was another room in the cellar – a small, dry-walled closet with electrical wires dripping down from the ceiling and two copper pipes protruding from the wall. More conduits that didn't lead anywhere. This room served as a mixed archive, taking in the overflow from the semblance of organisation that existed in other parts of the basement.

Lois started rooting through the bags and boxes that were closest. One shoebox was labelled 'Grandma/recipes'. She tugged at the box and immediately caused the downfall of their communal fuzzy felt collection. Pieces of soft space – stars, astronauts, black holes, galaxies – slow-motioned down to the floor, adhering to the concrete dust. After picking up the felt space bits, Lois peeked in the box. In between recipes for stargazy pie and beef wellington was a stack of letters, all of them addressed to Joan. She put the box in among the bottles.

Balancing the box on her knee, Lois closed the useless door and walked back up the concrete steps into the kitchen, which was humming with activity and smells and had been taken over by Maya and her mother. She walked over to the living room, where Gitsy was playing Boggle by herself on the coffee table.

'Look! I found it,' Lois said. 'My whisky collection!'

'What's whisky?' asked Gitsy.

The dining-room table was set around a stainless-steel tower that would soon accept the oysters that Nick was busy shucking on the balcony. Frank was neglecting the oysters in his office, probably writing to that woman, or about CDF, or falling down an escarpment in a part of the country he had never set foot in. She wasn't sure which of these was worse.

'Where's Wim?'

'He went over to Tara's,' said Maya.

'Where's Cole?'

'He's upstairs with the baby.'

Lois brought the two boxes to the Christmas tree. She went to the kitchen and filled her Peter Rabbit cereal bowl with ice. She took a tumbler from the dresser and returned to the tree. Behind the tree was a patch of floor where the underfloor heating was volcanic. She sat there and opened the box. The first thing that came out was a Talisker. She uncorked it and dropped a cube of ice into her glass as well a glug of the drink. She took her first sip. As the whisky fell down her throat she thought of the well shaft in Brittany, and how they would throw flaming newspapers down it for a few seconds of revelation.

Cole walked by with Finn in his arms and sat on the sofa. Lois looked at him through the low-hanging branches of the tree. He was playing round-and-round-the-garden on Finn's fat little palm. Finn's throaty laugh sounded like hiccups. At the far end of the room, Gitsy was spelling out her Boggle words.

'L-X-O-O-P-M-Y. How many points is that, Papa?'

'That's not a word, darling.'

'Yes, but HOW MANY POINTS?'

'It has to be a word that means something.'

'I'm not even playing that way,' she yelled. 'You don't even know how I'm playing.'

Finn observed with interest his defiant big sister. He and Cole had this look of admiration about them, a look Cole usually directed at Maya. Lois wondered whether Maya's infidelity could bring out a madness in Cole that no one suspected, least of all Maya. Seeing him on the sofa with the baby filled Lois with a sad envy. Nick was so far from reclining on a sofa with baby – a distance she had stretched out with her bad luck and bad choices.

She downed the rest of the whisky and took the lid off the shoebox. The label on the box indicated that it had once contained a pair of white perforated Dr Scholls. She took the first letter out. In the top-right corner of the envelope were a couple of Marianne stamps and the postmark for 13 October 1978.

Joni,

I can call you Joni? I think, Joni, I should like I kidnap you and bring you back here in the mountains, like I am the abominable snowman. I should like to build for you the perfect house. Buy for you a windsurf. Buy for you fresh flowers every morning. I know I am hirsute and a bad temper and the beast of your beauty. But I should like to convince you that I am not the waste of your time.

The letter was signed Frank. Lois didn't know what was more shocking – Joan's long-lost (and perhaps short-lived) nickname, or the fact that Frank had actually made the effort to write to her in English.

The next bottle to come out was a Lagavulin. As she poured her second drink, Simon walked to the Christmas tree and stared. She beckoned him into her spot. There wasn't much room behind the tree, so she made him lie down. 'Come and rub your growl on my temper,' she said. Simon slumped down and rested his paws on Lois's lap. His back fell against the French windows, stopping another draught from a ledge that was awaiting a stone trim.

Lois put the first letter back in the box and took out another.

Joni, I am counting the days to a day I know will be grand. I bought
a new picnic blanket for us. It is as you say fancy and rolls up into
the sausage with leather to close. I miss your Liberty nightdress
and your eyes, which are a shade of miracle.

Frank's efforts to communicate in English had in time
declined, and today his English voice was mostly used to
make fun of things it turned out were meaningful to Joan.
Joan said her husband's forays into the English language had
gone from unwonted to unwanted, a distinction that was of
course lost on Frank. It was strange to discover these letters
now, to hear Frank spellbound, labouring to seduce a woman
still uncommitted and pre-adaptation.

'Simon! Si-mon!' came Frank's voice from near the front
door. Frank rattled the leash and called again. Simon didn't
budge. Lois heard the front door close behind Frank. She put
her hand on the dog's neck and ruffled the fur there.

If I were to purchase a new bicycle for you, would you prefer it to be
blue or purple? I await your answer with bated breath.

This one was in French.

Lois ran her fingers along Simon's neck, starting at the
throat and going all the way to the point of his tooth that
hung over his bottom lip. Her back was pressed up against
the window, and the cold glass felt good against the heat from

the whisky. She watched as Maya and Joan got agitated in the kitchen, putting the final touches to the evening meal. Nick was smashing a bag of ice against the concrete planter on the balcony. She saw him swing the bag over his head and bring it down with a thud. Gitsy was now sharing Cole's lap with Finn, and both were concentrated on the Christmas story their dad was reading to them.

Lois pulled out a third bottle and dropped a second ice cube to work with the one that was half melted. Simon's head rolled back, and he gazed up at her with his upside-down puppy eyes. She rubbed his tummy. 'You look like a pilchard in a stargazy pie,' she said. Simon groaned his approval.

When he was done crushing ice and shucking oysters, Nick came over to the tree. 'I know you think it's cute to hide behind the Christmas tree and drink whisky, but it's not,' he said, his black apron spattered with grey slithers of shell. 'Why don't you come out and interact with your family.' He was including himself in 'family', she could tell.

Every now and again, Nick still wondered how much Lois had lied about the affair. If she'd fucked the Historian more than she had admitted to. If they'd ever left the city together to go somewhere. Upstate. Jersey. Somewhere stupidly close but far enough. He went through the soy sauce dishes, hunting for unfamiliar ones. He went looking for last year's calendar to see when they'd been apart, but last year's calendar wasn't in the file box with the other calendars. He wondered if she still thought of him. And if so, how often, and to what degree.

Lois knew Nick's forgiveness was not a done deal. It was, and would remain, a work in progress. She had told him she didn't miss the affair, and mostly it was true. Before long, she forgot the details she'd seen as cornerstones to her secret garden, moments she thought of as haunt-worthy vanished entirely, until all she could remember was a face her lover had once made when she'd used the wrong word for something. It was a face empty of commitment, a face that started and ended with judgement, a face whose preoccupations lay elsewhere.

'I'm turning into my dad,' thought Lois. She felt what it was like to be on the sideline and prefer the view from there. She imagined the Historian had fielded similar requests for participation from his wife. 'Are you going to be staring at your phone all night, or are you going to help us paint these Easter eggs?' his wife might have said. 'Are we boring you?' Good God, her father would have loved the Historian. They could have talked about the Occupation till the cows came home. Frank would have broken his people fast for him.

She watched Nick walk back to the kitchen and start slicing lemons. She knew him so well, she thought, that she could feel the sensation of the kitchen tiles under his feet just by looking at him. Gitsy had migrated from the sofa to the kitchen table. She cradled her cup of warm milk and looked up at her Uncle Nick like he was a god.

Lois sank back into the warmth of the dog, whisky and the

underfloor heating. From her sanctuary she stared at Nick, and found him responsible for her disfigurement. With his forgiveness and expectations he had cauterised the wound that kept her thinking, that kept her invested in the part of the world that wasn't him, or them. Nick, with all his love and advice and his lemons, was just another warlord.

8. Christmas Eve

'Sometimes I feel like I've spent the last three decades of my life not strangling you,' Joan told Frank as she adjusted his Christmas tie – tiny candy canes floating in the black void of space.

'Better not to start a conversation with "I've spent the last three decades of my life",' said Frank. 'People might think you were overstating. Or single-minded.'

'You're right. I wouldn't want people to think I was the obsessive sort,' retorted Joan.

In the hallway, Maya and Lois were play-squabbling over a missing hairbrush.

'Do me a favour, will you?' she asked.

'What?'

'I want you to make a sacrifice tonight.'

'Which one of them do you want me to get rid of?'

Joan walked over to their bathroom. Frank watched in the mirror as his wife dabbed perfume behind her ears with the glass stopper from the bottle. These rituals still fascinated him. For example: how did a woman know to dab it behind her ears? Was it a gesture she'd learned from her mother? Or was there a moment in a woman's life when she was taught the physics behind it – why it was more potent dabbed there and not, say, on the collarbone.

In the mirror and in her black dress, surrounded by the gauzy steam of an earlier shower, Joan looked like a bit like *The Wanderer Above A Sea Of Fog*. She slapped something white and creamy on her hands and ran them through her short blonde hair. Frank looked at Joan's face in the mirror, and caught her in the act of not looking back at him. She frowned to apply her lipstick – another enigma to Frank.

Joan walked back into the bedroom and put on her black patent slippers with the small gold buckle. It reassured him to see that her black slippers were still around, that the varnish on them wasn't scuffed, that they lived in a box and came out now and again. As long as the black slippers came out, things couldn't be that bad.

Frank went up to Joan and tried to put his arms around her. She moved towards the mirror and put on some earrings he thought might have been a gift from him.

'I want you not to write to your girlfriend until after Christmas.'

Frank felt the useless words follow the exit sign in his brain. Felt as they opened a trapdoor in the palate, endured the slow passage of the useless words into his buccal cavity. They moved slowly, like a fishbone falling in slow motion down the throat, bouncing from wall to wall before finding a fleshy part to anchor itself into. The useless words piled up at the door of his mouth, and the jam in his throat made him gag. It was obvious the useless words would go no further, would remain useless only to him, which was perhaps just as well.

Joan looked at him and knew exactly how uncomfortable she'd made him feel. She imagined the pathetic excuses he was sifting through in his mind, searching for the most credible one. How tedious to know this man so well, and be working at this alone. And – how risible to be worrying about his heart rate at a time like this.

Frank could see what she was thinking and was on her side. For two people who had stopped fulfilling each other's needs a while back, they were uncannily attuned to one another. Joan swept away an invisible speck on Frank's shoulder and walked out in front of him.

So she knew. Of course, he knew she knew. She had accepted his withdrawal, this was only the name of the withdrawal. Frank felt the tremendous urge to run after Joan and tell her that it meant nothing, that he loved her, that writing to H was pure buffoonery and that he would stop immediately.

He longed for her to walk back in the room and explain

the next steps to him. Give him one of her month-by-month planners, with relationship goals and goals around the house. By the end of January, I want you to have made an appointment with that therapist you were seeing. By mid-February, you are to empty the pool. By March, the bamboos have to be trimmed. I want new tenants in the office by mid-March, and at least 80 per cent of the archive shredded. He wanted to hear that she'd given this a lot of thought, and needed no convincing: she was cross with him, yes, but she'd give him another chance.

The words 'back-up plan' invaded his mind.

Frank turned out the light in their bedroom, closed the door and walked out into the corridor, the noise and warmth of his family rising up from the kitchen.

*

Lois spiked a tray of espressos with the dregs of the mystery Calvados and relegated the empty bottle to the box of recycling, where it stood among the corpses of the other, unmysterious bottles the family had consumed this Christmas. Earlier, Nick told her she drank too much. 'I'm not drunk, I'm sleepwalking,' she replied, smiling her flirtiest tipsy smile.

Lois took one of the cups up to the study, where Frank was sitting at his desk.

'It's Christmas Eve. You can't write your blog.'

'Everyone else here gets to do what they want.'

'Everyone else wants to do family stuff,' said Lois. 'Besides, we need your computer for karaoke.'

'I need to log out of my email.'

Lois stood in the doorway, watching her father.

'What are you doing?' Frank asked.

'Waiting for you to log out of your email.'

'I'll bring it down in five minutes.'

'I don't understand. What is your email? How involved is the logging-out process?'

'Why can't you use your own computer?'

'Because mine doesn't play DVDs,' said Lois.

'I'll bring it down.'

Lois left him to it.

Frank continued to delete emails from Heide. Some of them he opened up one last time, highlighting in his mind the bits he might want to recall in the future, one day when he felt like a lost cause. Some of them he knew almost by heart – lines that had made him flush, admissions that made him feel like he had something, anything to offer. Nothing, not one thing, had been asked of him, which suggested to him that what he gave covered all bases. It had been a good feeling while it lasted.

When the emails were all gone, he emptied the trash. Then he blocked her. Then he suspended his Facebook account. Then he deleted his history. 'From the beginning of time?'

From the beginning of time. Then he logged out of his email and carried the computer down to the basement, where the kids had made a clearing in a nook that was piled high with one-day tiles and punctured bicycle tyres no one had ever bothered to patch.

William plugged his speaker into the laptop.

'Wait, we have to enshrine it,' said Lois.

She unpacked the props she had brought down – Joan's blue velvet scarf, a string of leftover fairy lights, two plastic pomegranates, a tarot deck. Maya, who was sitting on a dusty brown bean bag in the corner of the room, felt feverish. She thought of Liz's cold fingers on the back of her neck.

After visiting Liz's farmhouse for the first time, Maya had an almost irresistible desire to rip out the white carpets in her own house. Take a box-cutter to the green upholstery on the new sofa. Drag the laminated white bookcases into the yard and bring a heavy axe down on them. She felt silly for surrounding herself with these things in the first place. For submitting to the notion that a home could be furnished in such a way as to make it seem complete, permanent. The farm had earned its features through the years, its orchard had matured over generations. She longed to bring Liz to Brittany, to show her the house that no one ever touched. How well it would reflect on her that this was also part of who she was.

She wondered whether her phone had died yet, or if it was still throbbing with incoming messages from Liz – a tiny blue beacon in a field of frozen cow manure. It always hit her once the kids were tucked in, just how much she missed Liz. If only she could split herself in two according to the hours of the day. A 7 a.m. to 7 p.m. Maya for the kids and Cole, and a night Maya. Night Maya wanted to tell Lois that no one actually wanted to sing along to Kate Bush in the basement. That it was just another indulgence that benefited her insular vision.

It was of course Lois who decided years back that singing along to *Hounds of Love* from beginning to end would make it onto the list of yuletide family lore. It was the album Joan liked to listen to at full volume when she was vacuuming the house, back when they still had a record player. The record player was somewhere in the promised wine cellar, broken and smothered by the other debris of their advancing lives.

William and Lois started to murder 'Running Up That Hill', reading the lyrics that scrolled across the lower third of a YouTube video. Frank, who was sitting on the bottom step, tapped his foot in time to his tic and, to a lesser extent, in time to the music. He made a mental note to speak to William tomorrow. A one on one. He'd ask him about school, and if he was managing financially. He'd suggest William get in touch with his client in Dubai. Maybe he could get an internship in his firm's Swiss office.

When the song ended, Lois grabbed Frank's hand and tried to pull him up from his seat.

'You sing one,' she ordered.

'I don't think so.'

'You really should try and get out of your comfort zone.'

Living is out of my comfort zone, thought Frank. Where would you have me go?

William searched for 'Hounds of Love', and muted the computer through an ad for a family SUV. 'Isn't that your car?' Lois asked Maya. The dig made Maya think about sex with Liz – how, after she parked her car, with its twin car seats and juice-carton graveyard, she and Liz fell into an immaterialism Lois could only dream about. She too could make selfish decisions that could later be deemed inevitable.

The song started, and William turned up the volume all the way. Cole walked over to the computer. 'My turn,' he said, taking Joan's velvet scarf and wrapping it into a bow around his head. It was already the most un-Cole moment any of them had ever witnessed, and he hadn't even sung a note yet. Maya stood up and gestured that she was going to check on the children.

Cole was singing loudly, miming a telephone call, pretending the love hounds were on the line. Lois joined in, massaging Simon's drooly cheeks with her hands. Frank looked at his son-in-law incredulously. William was in stitches. Nick looked around the room for an excuse, anything, to get up and do something. But there were no cups that needed refilling. No other people's children for him to check up on. No window somewhere upstairs that could be closed to stop a draught they all pretended not to notice.

*

After karaoke, Simon followed Lois up the stairs and to her bedroom. Lois slumped down on the bed and hitched her dress up around her hips. She lifted up her ass like a table to pull down her tights. She had to contort quite a bit to get them off, tugging in the places where she found no slack. She threw her tights in the air, and they came to land by Simon. The tights on the floor looked like a map of see-through black vales, black crevasses and soft gauzy peaks. Simon looked at them as intently as Frank surveyed his maps for 'bors'. Lois pulled her dress over her head and tossed that on the floor, too. The dress was like a puddle next to the tights. They were both still warm. It was incredible the way a woman could just separate herself from her warmth and her scent, thought Simon. Like shedding a coat, or losing a tail.

Lois walked across the room in her knickers, to the skylight. She opened it mechanically, and slid her hand into the space between the roof and the tiles, looking for a joint from the past. She found nothing.

As she walked back to the bed, she noticed Simon staring at her from the floor.

'What are you looking at?' she asked.

'You,' thought Simon.

Lois got into bed and buried herself under the blanket like a marmot.

'You can come and sleep on the bed if you want.'

Simon walked out of the room and slumped down outside the open door like a guard dog.

*

Upstairs in his bedroom, William was watching the cloud-tank video he'd made in his last year of senior school. The tank once belonged to Tara's older brother. Back then it was filled with sawdust, and housed a long white rat with pink eyes. When the rat died, Tara's mother took over the tank for one of her terrariums. Eventually it ended up in the brother's hands again, containing for a while his efforts to germinate cannabis seeds.

William had walked up and down the stairs to the basement carrying pots of boiled saltwater – not unlike Joan during Boilergate. He'd used up Joan's reserves of kosher salt, and switched the basement lightbulbs for black ones. As he emptied the saltwater into the tank, he might have heard Joan and Frank arguing upstairs. One of those silence-filling arguments about nothing at all. These had become more frequent since Maya moved out.

Later that night, he cut open a bin bag and laid it over the saltwater. He poured fresh water over the bag, working to make the stream from the jug as thin as possible. Joan had gone to bed, and Frank was snoring in front of a rerun of *NYPD Blue*. Delicately, Wim removed the sheet of polyethylene. He squeezed a drop of blue food colouring into the water. The colour expanded like a bruise, turning the water into sky.

He checked the camera and closed the basement door on Frank's snoring. The curtain of untrimmed ivy that dripped down from the first-floor planters blotted out any light from the outside world. Funny how he'd claimed the basement, all those years ago. First for his Egyptological expeditions, then for his Matchbox cars, and later as a film studio. He realised he must have spent more time down here than all of them combined.

He let rain a few drops of condensed milk into the tank, and they fluffed out into a perfect mammatus formation. He waited for the clouds to dissipate and added a few more. Next he sprinkled some glitter over the tank. The particles trickled through the sky, a slow-motion shower of cirrocumulus.

One of his earliest memories was of looking into the night sky, his parents' and his sisters' faces up there among the stars staring back down at him. Whenever his sisters pointed to the stars, with that incredible control they had of their limbs and hands, it seemed as though they were touching them. He had other memories of their sky-chasing excursions – in the mountains, in Brittany, with gas stoves, with blankets... But those came later, and by then he knew it had been a trick of perception, that the stars were too far away to feel, and that the last sky chase was too far back in the past to truly remember.

The clouds that piled up in the tank had nowhere to go. William poked the storm to life with the end of a feather. He threw in more glitter, which cut through the fog like clear rain. Then he sat down and waited. Waited for the tank to empty itself of atmosphere, to become still and dark again like the basement.

Later he added a soundtrack mixed from some old tape recordings of Lois and Maya that dated back to the early 1990s. An eight-year-old Lois reciting Villon's 'Ballad of the Hanged Men' in dribs and drabs for Frank's amusement, Maya two years younger, arguing for her fair share of the Fisher Price mic. Odd to hear his sisters chatting away, back when he didn't have words yet, was still just a lovable pudding that got passed around and goo-goo-gahed at.

He'd been given an A+ for the film. Not that it counted towards much. Frank and Joan were impressed. So was Tara. The tank had also left its mark on the basement floor.

Lying in bed tonight, William thought he could hear Nick talking to someone downstairs. He closed his eyes. He would go down to the basement tomorrow. See if the tank was still around. When he opened his eyes again, he was looking at Tara through condensed milk, his laser-beam eyes catching glimpses of her in the space between the milky atoms. His sisters were there too. They were all swimming in milk. He could see everything so clearly. The lake still. The sky placid. Everything as it should be.

*

Simon would have to play it carefully with Lois. He had to give Frank what he wanted, which was the illusion of his loyalty. Illusion because, while Simon liked Frank a lot, and could possibly even be loyal to him of his own accord, the circumstances of dependency he found himself in meant that he could never find out. Talk about holding something so close it suffocates.

Humans act worse than gods. They act like parents. They see you and they decide you are theirs. An extension of their breed. They pick you out, they brand you with their instruction and then demand that you love them back.

They put you in situations of need to stimulate this love. They keep you away from food that runs, and close to food that sits in tins and needs to be opened by machines operated by human hands. They put you in places with doors that lock and can only be opened by keys held by human hands. They expect you to piss on schedule, and to extend the love you owe them to the people *they* love. They annihilate your discretion, even as they train you to be discreet.

They subdue your nature. They take your desire to run and they contain it. Give it a timetable. They put your love of the outdoors on a leash. They purchase equipment for your needs that you must then create needs for. So they can feel good about the money they spent on you.

They make your life comfortable in an old-person way, starting when you are a puppy. They get irritated when the mud that sets in between your claws on the walks they take you on shakes off onto the clean floor. They don't like it that you shed hair, and they complain loudly and often about how much hair you shed. Meanwhile, they remind their children it is impolite to comment on others' appearance.

Your mutual arrangement is two contracts pretending to be one. Your crate is their power of attorney. Your loyalty is their demand for your loyalty. Their affection is real, but it comes with strings attached. Strings that lead to collars and vaccines and tin openers, and kennels where different hands will open the same brand of dog food if your owners decide to go on holiday.

For the most part, how you will relate to them from now until you die is unnatural. And don't forget – you will most probably die at the hour of their choosing. Your death will occur in full consideration of their work schedule, prior commitments, etc. You will die if and only if the car starts that day. If the car doesn't start that day, your exit appointment will be postponed. If the vet is not too busy that day curing or dispatching some other creature with atrophied joints or other conditions with no room for improvement. The fuckers are fine with euthanasia when it comes to you, but still grapple with it for themselves.

And yet there are days when your relationship will transcend its foundation of mutual – if weighted – servitude. Master and dog will run together into a cold mountain brook on a hot afternoon in August. Dog and master will snore in unison in front of the fireplace in a house in Brittany, and later eat snacks at an inappropriate hour. Both will enjoy a cut of ham from the same pig's hindquarter. In these rare moments you are two creatures, two beings, playing out their independence side by side.

Simon had enjoyed such moments with Frank. And, to a lesser extent, with Joan.

With Lois, everything was different.

For starters, she did nothing for him. Or rather, she did nothing for him with a purpose. The last time she was here, Frank and Joan drove to Italy for the weekend. Joan left a list of instructions that read like a dog manual. Lois used the back of the list to scribble something down and never looked at it again. She forgot to put out biscuits for him, but fed him scraps off her plate. Eventually she took the lid off the biscuits, and let Simon determine his own mealtimes. She slept in late and didn't walk him first thing in the morning as instructed. Instead, she slept with the French windows open all night.

It was on the night of the storm that he fell for her. That day, Frank and Joan left a message on the answerphone saying they were staying in Turin a second night. First the rain came. It tripped off the roof and onto the copper ledge, keeping them both awake. Then came the thunder, making the mountain behind them groan. At one point, lightning struck a tree and she yelled his name.

She hadn't parcelled out his meals, or anticipated when he might need to piss or take a shit. In fact, she'd done nothing for him all day. And now she needed him. Screamed her need for him in a house with no parents. She closed all the doors on them that night, and Simon did not leave the side of her bed until morning.

He liked that she was a slob. She had short hair which she seldom washed. She wore anyone's socks – whatever was lying around. She stole clothing from the others. Underwear from Maya. Socks from Gitsy. Sweaters from everyone. She seemed to be lacking that notion of ownership that they all had. With her, he felt safe. Expropriated.

He noticed that she touched him more than she touched her husband. She used Simon to get away from Nick. 'Dog needs a walk,' she'd say. 'I'll take him.' He liked being used this way.

Last night, when he was sitting at her feet, the idea came into his head again to bite her. Not hard, not to draw blood, but to see the shape of his teeth on her ankle. To know he'd moved her flesh around, put a him-shaped dent in it. He didn't know what else to do to her.

He said this to her. Simon said, 'I want to eat your heart right out of you, I want to cock my head so I can lick the side of your foot from heel to toe.' When he opened his mouth to feel her foot, she extended her toe right into it. She didn't seem to find him either adorable or repulsive. Was this what it was like to be a man? Or was this what it felt like to be a happy dog? Either way, he couldn't get enough of it.

*

Nick had just finished loading the dishwasher when he remembered it hadn't worked in years. He filled the sink with hot water and squirted some washing-up liquid into it. He plunged the glasses in. It felt good to drown his hands like this. From the sink he could see the house without its occupants. There were parts that were Joan, like the collection of antique green-glass vases on the windowsill, the oversized cookbooks with attractive spines and ribbon bookmarks, and the photos of the kids. There were parts that were Frank, like the sticking-out wires and sudden concrete edge, or the lack of a handrail on the stairs.

He wondered what Frank was really doing in his office. When he was shucking the oysters, Cole had advanced that Frank might be writing a memoir. 'Who cares?' Wim had said.

The automatic light came on outside, casting a limp white glow on the wall. Nick heard footsteps coming up the stairs and the front door open. Simon trotted into the kitchen and went straight to his food bowl. Wim's girlfriend Tara was on his heels.

'He was in our garden,' she said, in her perfect English, with her perfect fuck-you French accent. 'My parents get cross because of that.'

'And about the bamboos.'

'You heard about the petition.'

'Yes,' said Nick. 'Those bamboos are a force of God. Your parents are either very powerful or very naive.'

Simon walked out of the kitchen and went to sit in the patch where Lois had polished off the dregs of her whisky collection several hours earlier. He licked an invisible spot where she had sat on the marble tiles.

'I was going to make tea,' said Nick. 'Do you want some?'

'No. But I'll take a cigarette.'

Nick took the pack of cigarettes out of his shirt pocket and handed it to Tara.

'Wim went to bed a bit ago,' he said. 'I don't know if he's asleep.'

Tara grabbed the matches by the stove and walked out onto the balcony. Nick followed her and put a cigarette in his mouth. The garden table still smelled briny from the oyster-shucking. The smell was so intense it made him feel self-conscious.

'So what do your people do at Christmas?'

'We eat a goose, and my parents watch television.'

'Is there a reason we didn't see you here tonight?'

Tara made a smoke ring in the air and tried to shoot another ring through the first one. When she failed, she giggled.

'He broke up with me.'

'That boy is a young, young idiot,' said Nick.

Nick had always wondered about their relationship. Tara seemed so worldly. William was a lamb. It wouldn't have surprised him to hear Tara had broken it off. She was the kind of girl who would have a certain world at her feet in the foreseeable future. The last thing she needed was a twenty-one-year-old senior-school sweetheart who lived in London with room-mates.

Simon pushed open the door with his nose, and came to sit on the floor between them. Nick was surprised at how warm the dog felt against his calf.

'Do you think if you are in love when you're eighteen, you are doomed?' asked Tara.

'No.'

'But it is inconceivable you will stay together.'

'Precisely.'

Tara's hair smelled of incense and gravy. On the other side of the lake, someone let off a couple of red and blue fireworks. Simon barked quietly, out of duty.

Just then, Tara leaned in and kissed him. Nick was about to tell Simon to shut up, and the kiss suffocated the first syllable of the dog's name, which came to die on her lips. It was a diminutive kiss that barely registered on a tactile level.

Tara pulled away and threw her legs out in front of her. The heels of her boots went thump on the cold concrete floor. Nick lifted the cigarette back to his mouth and said, 'Well, shit.'

'Well, shit,' echoed Tara.

Lazy drops of snow started to fall on the table. Simon made his way to the door and wagged his tail to be let in.

'I should go,' she said.

'All right.'

Tara got up and walked back inside with Simon. Nick heard the front door close behind her. The house was silent. Even Frank was asleep.

9. Christmas Day

THE NIGHT BEFORE Christmas was like a spell. The wait for Christmas morning lasted only a few hours of sleep, but the night's enchantment stretched out those few hours like the rolling pin her grandma used to roll out the shortcake lids for the mince pies. Gitsy knew this to be true because she had more dreams on Christmas Eve than on any other night of the year. An average of five dreams, each with their own plot and back story.

This year again, Gitsy had gone to bed on the 24th feigning obedience. She didn't protest when her grandma tucked her in and kissed her goodnight. She closed her eyes and stayed very still for a few minutes after her mum turned out the lights, in case Maya was waiting by the door for proof of sleep. She listened for the grown-ups' footsteps to disappear down the stairs, counted up to one-hundred-Mississippi, and got out of bed in the dark. With her hand she followed the wall all the way to the window and found the light switch. Earlier, she'd stashed the *Jolly Postman* book and some clementines under the bed to keep her alert until the Great Man showed up. This year, she vowed to stay awake.

The Christmas spell was powerful. You could try to outsmart it and stay awake, but eventually the charm knocked you out. At 11.22 p.m., Gitsy's eyelids would no longer stay open. She allowed herself a catnap. She would rest her eyes ever so briefly, and still wake up in time to catch Santa coming down the chimney – the one that hovered over nothing, over an absent fireplace that contained the possibility of future memories. Perhaps this year Santa would bring a fireplace.

Dream number one kicked in. Something about reindeers and clementines. Followed by dream number two, which involved Finn being naughty. On its heels, dream number three. In one of the dreams her parents had a raging fight. Her mum threw something at the painting in the living room, which tore a hole in the canvas. She made it to a record six before something told her it was morning, and that the spell had weakened enough that she could drag herself out of slumber if she tried hard enough.

Gitsy sat up in bed. She was the only one with any willpower in this house. The others were still under the spell, and would be so for an interminable amount of time – probably until 8 a.m. There was clementine peel on the pillow and a few squished segments on the sheet. She swept the sticky pieces under the pillow. She got out of bed, put on her slippers and opened the bedroom door.

On the landing she heard Frank snoring in Grandma's bedroom.

Halfway down the stairs, Gitsy sat on a step to wake up properly. It occurred to her she had better check that she was, in fact, awake, and that this wasn't simply dream number seven. She pinched herself, but she couldn't tell if it hurt or not. Someone was asleep on the brown pinstripe sofa and had covered themselves with the itchy white blanket that Simon sometimes slept on. There was a fricative snore coming from the person, which closer inspection revealed to be Uncle Nick.

Simon appeared out of nowhere and nudged Gitsy for his feed. Gitsy went over to the big box of dog biscuits and prized the lid off with both hands. Simon put his head inside the box and ate.

The Christmas tree with its blinking lights was a shocking sight. There was a wide moat of presents under the tree, and the stacks also grew vertically. Gitsy looked for her name on all the tags, and then for Finn's. The mince pie was gone from the plate she'd left out for Santa, as was the letter she'd written him, asking him those practical questions about his existence that still bothered her. He'd also downed the brandy.

'Uncle Nick.'

Uncle Nick didn't move, but she knew he was awake because the snoring had stopped.

'I know you're awake.'

'I'm not awake yet,' said the itchy white blanket.

'Can I have cereal?'

'Ask your parents.'

'They're sleeping. They'll be cross if I wake them up.'

Nick sat up on the sofa.

'Why did you go to sleep in your clothes?'

'Because I couldn't find my PJs.'

'Why didn't you look in your room?'

Nick walked over to the kitchen and poured some Cheerios into a bowl. He placed the bowl on the table.

'Can I have a spoon?'

He grabbed a spoon from the dish rack and handed it to Gitsy.

'Milk?'

'You know, when I was your age,' said Nick, 'I had to make dinner for my whole family.'

'That's what Mum says. But I checked with Grandma and it's not true.'

Gitsy took her cereal to the tree and Nick walked out onto the balcony. The door closed behind him, locking him out. He picked up the cigarette butts from last night and a champagne flute that had neatly broken in two. He remembered Tara's face next to his, just before she turned it, and flinched. Inside,

Joan was leading Gitsy and her cereal back to the kitchen table. He knocked at the window to be let in.

'You're up early' said Joan.

'He couldn't find his pyjamas,' said Gitsy.

Joan took off her wedding ring and put it on the windowsill. She rubbed cream into her hands and up to her elbows. Nick turned on the kettle for coffee.

'Can I open a present?' asked Gitsy.

'I think we should wait for the others to wake up,' said Joan.

'How about you open just one?' said Nick. 'You can open mine.'

'What does it look like?'

'Like a spherical night light that projects constellations onto the ceiling,' he said.

Joan looked for some dirty dishes to wash from last night, but couldn't find any. She wondered whether Heide had sent Frank Christmas wishes, and what they might sound like. She wondered if he'd checked his email. They had barely spoken since their conversation in the bedroom, but Frank had been unusually present all night. Not attentive, just in the way.

'Grandma, come and see!'

Gitsy's nose was pressed against the living-room window. The garden was white and getting whiter. The trenches, the jutting bamboo hedge, the piles of rubble – it had all vanished under an invisibility cloak of snow.

Nick plugged Gitsy's new night-sky projector in. The globe

spun round in silence, casting invisible stars onto the snow-white ceiling.

*

The branch that had once looked like a pokey witch finger had grown, and now poked right past the window, pointing to something in the distance that couldn't be seen from the bed. The cotton-boll-grey sky through the window suggested it was snowing lightly. In the cot, Finn's little chest went up and down like it ought to.

Maya grabbed the cup of water next to the bed, but it was empty. Cole inched closer to her under the quilts and wrapped his leg around hers. Liz knew nothing about this kind of living – this having children to wake up for in the morning, and all decisions split down the middle. Liz and her lovely, ignorant freedom. Perhaps Liz was exercising her freedom right now, in Turkey, with her co-worker. Maybe Liz's legs were wrapped around her colleague's legs, in a bed that would be remade while they sat on the patio in robes, eating their complimentary Continental breakfast.

Cole buried his head into Maya's neck so he could kiss it. She stretched her fingers around his knee, holding it like an apple. How round and steady his knee was, she thought. Nothing like her father's febrile knee and febrile everything, drawing all the attention to itself but not giving anything back. She stroked Cole's thigh. She thought of how much more difficult things would be if Cole wasn't like Cole – if he didn't make things as comfortable and reassuring as Cole made them. It was one thing to escape hardship, another to question your enviable reality.

Now Cole was hard, and lying on top of her. Now he was moving his head to kiss the other side of her neck. She kissed him too, when his skin presented itself to her mouth. Now he was undoing the buttons on her nightshirt. It was one of those masculine nightshirts that were meant to make you feel sexy without even trying. Maya tried to think of Liz, who made her feel sexy without trying. She tried to imagine the semi-familiar body of Liz, but couldn't conjure up a precise image of her. Instead she saw the absence of Liz, in Cole's presence, and felt it, and felt him, like the dull beat of a battering ram against a castle door.

Afterwards, Cole got up to fill the empty water glass in the upstairs bathroom. Maya got up and opened the window, and buried herself under the covers once more. Joan would do this, in the middle of winter – open their bedroom windows all the way even if it was Baltic outside. It woke up your face and your brain, even as your body stayed sleep-mummified under the blankets. Maya sometimes rolled the covers down, inch by inch, to awaken the other lazy parts of her. First the neck, then the shoulders, then the heart.

'You were talking in your sleep last night,' said Cole.

'Was I?' said Maya.

Another Lois trait. She'd better watch herself.

Cole put the glass down by the bed and went to get Finn, who was cooing through his pacifier.

'It was sort of entertaining once I started paying attention to what you were saying.'

'What did I say?'

'It didn't make much sense. You mentioned Gitsy, and water. Stuff about an apron? And then you got really pissed off.'

'At who?'

'Not sure. But whatever it was, it was making you really angry, like someone was doing you a tremendous injustice.'

Cole handed Finn to Maya. He immediately went burrowing in her effortlessly sexy nightshirt, which was still open from earlier.

'Here, take him for one sec,' she said to Cole. 'I'm going to make him a bottle.'

Finn started crying when Cole took him away. Maya sat up on the edge of the bed and pulled on her woolly white socks.

Over the years, whenever she felt Cole slipping away, she conjured up that one time he'd saved her life. It was impossible to know for sure whether he had saved her life that day, since the only thing that could prove a deadly risk was death itself. But everyone seemed to agree that he had, that summer in Brittany when she forgot to count the waves in sevens and got sucked into the undertow. Cole was too good, much too good to imagine he'd ever profited from that debt.

'You were also mumbling about Liz.'

'Liz?'

'Yes.'

Maya fished last night's bottle out of the cot and walked out of the bedroom, followed by Cole and Finn.

'Maybe it was a swimming dream,' he said. 'I used to get those when I was in therapy.'

Downstairs, Gitsy was yapping away to Joan.

'Maybe,' said Maya.

*

If Simon marked his territory by pissing, Nick was marking his by not letting him piss. He'd been standing by the door for ten minutes, and still Nick refused to open it. Simon knew that if he pissed on the floor it would reflect poorly on Nick, not him. Still, it would underline his impotence and it would be he who suffered the embarrassment. There are few things as off-putting in life as an incontinent dog on Christmas morning.

Simon assumed that Nick was angry because he had slept in his bedroom, next to his wife, while Nick slept on the couch. Of course, it wasn't Simon's fault that Nick had slept on the couch. There was nothing for him to usurp. You didn't cross over into another physical world just because your heart did. In many ways, Nick's jealousy was the highest validation Simon's feelings would ever get. The rest – it just felt like locked-in love syndrome. There was no future for a lovesick dog.

The only thing Lois and Simon would ever be able to join, in public, on a Christmas morning like this one, was their resignation. Her understanding that she could not become his mistress, and his stoicism over the knowledge that she was not to be had by him. In this respect, he supposed, they were unified in their own way. Their relationship was articulated around walking, lying or sitting – it was devoid of any other concern, practicality or desire. With them there were no goals. Perhaps that was what Nick resented. To have no hopes for a model love from the start. With Simon, there were no such ambitions, so Lois could successfully not meet them.

And then there was the question of until death do us part. Simon's seven-year lifespan removed any burdensome aspiration of perpetuity. A dog was not for life. Not like a Nick.

Sometimes Simon felt like they were two children at summer camp. They were flung together in their new shorts and sensible sandals, and for a week ate breakfast together every day and held hands as they walked to the park, and everyone knew which ones were their seats around the campfire. For a while it looked as if they would eat breakfast and hold hands and sit together for ever. But then camp ended and they each went their own way and exchanged phone numbers and said they would see each other next year, but even at their age they could feel how fast they were changing, and that there was no guarantee that, even if they did meet again next year, they would want to sit next to each other at the breakfast table or in front of the fire.

'Why do I do this?' thought Simon. 'Translate everything into human?' Perhaps it was because they translated everything into dog for him. Even the things he could perfectly grasp in their human iteration. They must think he was stupid. That he didn't notice things. But Joan talked to herself in front of him, Frank picked his nose, Maya texted her girlfriend… In their eyes, he was not a credible witness. He was a walking, barking thing of no consequence.

Simon knew that he wouldn't kill himself over her. Not that he didn't feel desperation. He did. But he had also to accept that he had a stronger response to Joan fetching his leash and saying 'Walkies!' than to this other situation. Besides, any thought of suicide was clouded with the stress of knowing how to do it, how on earth to find a process that could be controllable by a beast like him, and efficient at the same time. The thought made him leaden. Whereas the mention of a walk and the promise of a bone-shaped peanut-butter treat still made him want to jump up and bound to the door. That is why their love was perfect – he would probably never lose actual sleep over her because his instincts drove him despite his better judgement. He would never want to die from love, because while he was wired for suffering, he was too distracted to be properly morbid.

Like right now: upstairs was a woman he had come to love, and he would like the ownership of him to shift from Frank to her, and he was mulling this over in his head, but also he had a strong desire to run into the garden, piss on the bamboos, and then roll in the snow until his tail was cold. And he might – he thought – he just might want that more.

*

The first to raise an objection was the butcher. He wiped two bloody hands on his starched white apron, and said that the proof was in the pudding. Joan wondered whether he meant black pudding or pudding, as in dessert. She hated black pudding – the thick smell of blood evaporating in oil. The way apples cooked in the same pan turned to protein. Frank's sister always made it for him when she came to visit. Sat him down and watched him eat until his plate was clean, like a baby.

'Once a cheat, always a cheat,' said the woman who was carrying an infant in her yellow shawl. Joan tried to remember the figurine's catalogue description. Was it 'Mother'? Perhaps she had just been labelled 'Woman'. The baby in the shawl had bouncy pink cheeks, just like Finn.

'I say get out while you can,' said the woman. This confused Joan. Why would she not be able to get out in the future? What, aside from the vows of marriage, could keep her tied to Frank against her will? Guilt, perhaps.

'It's not like anything's happened yet,' said the knife sharpener. The clay wheel kept spinning under the clay blade of his clay knife as he said this, and Joan wondered whether it would in time disappear completely. 'We're talking emails. It's a fantasy. It's not even real letters.'

Joan had an inkling Frank had crossed into the analogue world, and sent some real letters too. The thought of him writing a love letter in his pathetic, stringy handwriting, licking an envelope, walking to the post office to purchase a stamp for the first time in years made her queasy. All that effort. All that effort that proved he still could, if he wanted to.

Once upon a time, he'd written her some letters. There was that one summer, after her term in Annecy, when she went back to England, to her parents' house, to weigh up her options. Frank wrote to her most days. Every day a letter would fall through the letterbox and land on the mat. Often she would see them cascading through the door from the kitchen table. Sometimes there'd be no letter for days but then a stack of them all at once. She organised them according to the ascending postmarks – not the order in which she received them – and hid in the garden shed to read them. She still had them somewhere. The letters were probably downstairs, in among the junk they collected, perhaps to prove to future generations they'd really been around at one point. That they'd really been good at that love thing.

One of the children came forth carrying a tray of heather corsages. 'You're an ENFJ,' she said. 'You're a strong, capable, empathetic woman. Repeat after me, Joan.'

'I'm a strong, capable, empathetic woman,' said Joan.

Lois walked past with a cup of coffee and sniggered.

'You should put the sweet potatoes in soon,' the clay child said. Or maybe it was Lois who had said that.

She would prepare as much as she could this morning, before they all came down and left their coffee cups lying around, and made eggs in five different pans that would need soaking five different ways.

Gitsy was unwrapping gifts in the living room, squealing with each new toy, explaining breathlessly what it did and how. Joan wondered whether Wim had unwrapped his sweater yet. She knew she had the receipt somewhere.

'Mum! Come and open your presents, you strong, capable, empathetic woman!' yelled Lois.

She didn't like the way Frank always got her the books he thought she should read. So condescending. But then again, that was the least of her problems these days. She would never have admitted it to them, but it pissed her off the way Lois never made an effort with presents at Christmas, like it was no big deal. It was just another matter that had been settled by the years. Lois didn't really try, and that was also part of Christmas. Joan always went out of her way to get the girls perfect gifts – small, useful luxuries that were 'so Maya' or 'so Lois'. Maya got her things like a blender, a crock pot or a magazine stand. Once upon a time, Lois had really, really known her. Had read her desires better than she herself could. Perhaps this year there was a crushed-velvet apron for her under the tree. A reminder that her children knew she had existed before all of them.

'If you forsake him now, you may live to regret it.'

It wasn't obvious at first where the voice was coming from.

'Of course, if you don't, you may die to regret it.'

In the sectioned paper-mâché barn, laid out on a pillow of genuine straw and flanked by his virginal mother and Jeanot, the village lush, was baby Jesus. Jeanot must have sleepwalked over to the manger in the night. Baby Jesus was looking straight up at her. The clay swaddling had been painted over with Tipp-Ex where it had chipped, and the baby's lips were so red, it looked as if he was wearing Joan's YSL Rouge Pur Couture.

Life, death and regret. And Christmas dinner cooked in a convection oven that was one of the most expensive ones on the market in 1998. And at least the door to the office had stayed closed this morning.

10. Capon

FRANK, WHO WAS suffocating in the sea of wrapping paper, curly satin ribbons and aromas from the flesh of the neutered fowl that was roasting in the kitchen, announced it was time to attack the day.

'Here we go,' growled Maya. Her second hangover headache in months was just starting to dissipate. 'Dad wants to lead us all down his personal warpath through the day.'

'Maybe for once you could see the day as something other than your personal enemy,' Joan chimed. 'It might even help with your blood pressure.'

Frank remembered the pills he'd forgotten in all the morning's activity. As per usual, he'd lined them up the previous day on the *Fliegende Hollander* CD case – 1959 Bayreuth recording. He swallowed down the pills with the last of the coffee, and took a clean pan from the cupboard to fry himself an egg. Joan sighed.

'Those of you who want to pretend that living is not about fending off impending death can also join me,' he said.

Gitsy, who was busy examining Simon's paw under her new telescope, looked up. 'Why did he say death?' Maya shot her father a look of death.

None of them got it. None of them had yet reached their best-by date. None of them felt like he did – a still-edible yogurt at the back of the fridge that no one wanted to touch. They weren't having to distract mortality with a saltless diet and pills. None of them had hearts that needed to be controlled with drugs. None of them felt the need to offset this control by letting their hearts roam a little wild.

Frank cracked the egg on the edge of the pan and held it together for a while over the spitting oil. Joan was acting as though last night had never happened. Frank wondered whether it meant that the last six months had never happened. He felt a lightness this morning from his digital untethering of the previous night, but at the same time he was wound up tight. The situation felt positively Brechtian.

He pushed the two halves of the shell apart and the egg flopped into the pan. The edges started to go white, and soon the whole thing hardened around the only part Frank liked soft.

*

After breakfast they piled into Maya's rental SUV and Frank's garbage car and drove down to the lake – a Christmas morning ritual for as long as anyone could remember. In the car, Simon's snout kept bumping up against the back of Lois's head through the headrest. Her hair felt like damp straw, but it smelled like Joan. Frank pointed to the mountain and asked Nick if he could see the lying woman. 'What is she lying about?' said Nick. There was an altar to the Virgin atop her left mountainous breast, said Frank. 'The best hike is where her hand – do you see her thumb, over there – rests against her thigh. You climb up her thumb and into her crotch, and then it's another hour's walk to her forehead,' said Frank.

Two years ago, Frank had found himself lost in her. When he didn't recognise the trail he turned back, but never managed to get back on the loop. By the time he found his car it was dark. When he got home he told Joan he had had dinner with a client, but the words came out defensive. 'What, are you having an affair?' she snorted. He laughed at the idea, too – to punish himself for being late, and to punish himself for being old. The next day Frank called his doctor and asked to be tested for Alzheimer's. The test had come out fine. The only thing to worry about, said the doctor, was his heart and cholesterol. That was when the privations were first introduced.

Age had shrunk Frank's playground. Once he had known

his way around blinding-white glaciers, navigated amateur climbers between invisible crevices. Today he couldn't find his way around the shape of a woman, and was outwalked by a pedigree dog with doomed joints.

Frank parked next to Cole and Maya, who was bundling up Finn and ordering Gitsy away from the icy puddles. Gitsy ran off to swing on the turnstiles.

The structure of this family, thought Frank, had something harebrained about it. The alignment of these wills and personalities, all in some common effort dictated by the rituals of dead people no one could even remember, was almost unnatural. It's not possible, he thought, that every one of us wants to be here this morning. And yet here we are.

It was what they did on Christmas morning. They had breakfast, Joan put things in the oven that had to stay in there for hours, and they went for a walk by the lake. They rarely patronised the beach in the summer, preferring to borrow a catamaran or rent a pedal boat, and swim where the water didn't have to be shared with others.

Once, Wim had gone to the beach with friends and opened his foot jumping off the diving board. He needed twelve stitches and a tetanus shot. As he recalled, the diving board was huge and terrifying. But today it looked piddly and ancient, with its rusty ladder and the mossy cracks in its waterslide.

Lois was wearing her mother's coat and was cocooned up to her nose in her mother's scarf. Simon was sticking to her like a limp. 'Simon!' yelled Frank, shaking a big stick. Simon ignored him. Frank felt conspicuous without his dog. Joan was talking to Maya by the water. He wondered whether they were talking about him. Whether Joan had told the children about him. He didn't think so. There hadn't been time.

'How's university?'

'Fine,' said Wim.

Frank tried to remember what year Wim was in, in case Wim quizzed him. That was the kind of cruel trick the children played on him every now and again. Asked him if he remembered their age, or birthdays, or other details. What did it prove, anyway? That they could be placed on a timeline? Frank had feigned ignorance about his own age for so long that some days he really wasn't sure.

'How's Tara?'

'I don't want to talk about it.'

Wim was by far the most unreadable of the three children. Lois was always betrayed by her behaviour or appearance, and Maya uttered every thought or feeling as though it were a dangerous weather alert.

'I have three essays that are due in March. I want to get them done this holiday.'

'Why?'

'So I don't have to stress out about it.'

'Yes. Don't be stressed now. None of the stressful part of life has started yet.'

The stressful part of life was getting lost in your own garden, making sure the chalet was ready in time for your wealthy client's skiing holiday. Waiting for Part Two of the you'rewritingtoanotherwoman conversation.

'Sometimes I think we live on the wrong side of the lake,' said Joan. 'It's much nicer on that side.' The other bank had the sun in its eyes and the road there was winding and picturesque. Theirs was the functional side, with the roadside supermarket, auto concessions and the bike lane. The other side had more whimsy, with green-grass beaches, listed abbeys and tall trees to obscure gardens that were really small parks.

'Of course, the one bad thing about that side of the lake is they have to look at us,' she said.

Frank ripped the stick out of Simon's jaw and threw it into the lake, as far as he could towards the other side.

*

Rinse capon out like you would a chicken and pat away excess moisture with paper towels. Rub with salt and stuff with preferred stuffing (sausage, chestnut and sage base plus apple, pear or orange zest). Add herbs (marjoram, tarragon or thyme). Stuff large bird at both ends: neck and cavity. Stop the stuffing with a medium-sized fruit or citrus (small apple, pear or lemon). Truss with twine and sear on all sides in large pan using butter. Place bird in deep roasting tin adding shallots, whole unpeeled garlic and parsnips. Cover with parchment paper. Baste often/generously for an all-over glaze. Serve with giblet and white wine gravy. Side dishes: potato (roasted, mashed or sautéed), watercress, devils on horseback, boiled carrots, creamed onions.

Joan wasn't sure which of the girls had found her mother's recipe cards, and stuck her instructions for roasting a capon to the refrigerator door. Lois, she guessed. Maya was more direct, more likely to create a small scene around such a find. There was a small brown stain in the top-right corner of the card in the shape of Saturn. Probably gravy. She thought of her mother thickening the gravy with cooking wine and minced giblets, before splashing it onto the index card. Joan rubbed the stain between her fingers and saw her mother at the sink. Her mother's white apron strings fell into the pleat of her woollen skirt. She turned to Joan and smiled, her hands foaming with big yellow bubbles from the new bar of Pears soap.

Joan had thought of her mother often in the last twenty years. How much her mother would have loved the house in Brittany, with its royal-blue shutters and Herculean blackberry hedge. What a kick she'd get out of Gitsy. How, if she'd been alive today, Wim could have visited at the weekend and taken her grocery-shopping at Morrisons. Joan thought of her mother in relation to the landscape and to the children, drawing wishful lines between her and those who didn't miss her as much as she did.

Looking at the stain today, she longed for her mother in a way that wasn't altruistic. Wanted to crawl head-first into her mother's itchy grey lap, and have her head stroked firmly like everything would turn out all right. Removing the yams from the oven, she thought of how cruel it was to be a mother without a mother of your own.

None of them ever bothered to check in with her. Including Lois, who still hadn't mentioned a thing about their phone conversation. In fact, Lois seemed to spend as much time on her computer as Frank these days. Like father like daughter, thought Joan, immediately regretting the thought.

As she basted the capon often/generously for an all-over glaze, she resolved one day to surprise, really surprise the fuckers.

*

Frank was full from dinner, even though he'd barely touched the food. Throughout the meal he'd tried to catch Joan's eye, complimenting her on the stuffing, and generally delivering over-eager punditry on the unfolding meal. Joan gave him no more – or less – attention than the others, as a consequence of which Frank had no idea what was going on in her head. On a practical level, he wasn't sure where to sleep tonight. He could hardly go upstairs and sleep next to Joan, pretend that nothing had happened. He considered the sofa, but the kids would likely be up all night again, drinking and being loud.

Frank went to the landing and dragged Simon's dog bed back to his office, just in case.

It had started snowing again. The snowfall killed any distance and perspective around the lake and made the world look four foot deep. A voluminous grey nothing hovered outside the window of Frank's office as he opened his computer. For the first time in months, his inbox was Heide-free. The urge to unblock her was tremendous. If he did, he wondered, would a number of unreceived emails get delivered all at once? Would he find anxious notes, asking what happened and was it something I said? Eventually he would have to write to Heide. Right now, though, he knew that scorning H's feelings was part of his atonement.

In his inbox was an email from the Dubai client for whom he had done a chalet renovation. From the outside the chalet was a pastoral Alpine postcard, but on the inside it was all poured concrete and severe angles. The client was renewing his invitation for Frank to visit Dubai and meet prospective chalet owners. 'Bring your wife,' the client had said. The image of Joan flying business-class to Dubai and being met at the airport by a chauffeur with a sign with their name on it filled him with reassurance. He told the client that he and his wife accepted the invitation, and would send over some possible dates to see if they were agreeable. After he replied to the client, Frank opened up an essay he was writing on the logic of branches in Friedrich's work.

Frank saw each branch as a silhouetted finger, pointing to some other, more exceptional corner of the landscape. Branches were roads on a map. Boughs and twigs spelled a route to a certain perspective. The flayed stump of an alder drove the gaze downwards to a mossy ravine. A fallen trunk was a footbridge over a bog, leading one to a better vantage point. The steadying sapling on the cliffs of Rügen permitted a closer look at the drop. Like any other 'bor' searched for on a map, the heart of the painting was a thing to be reached. Bor as heart: the idea pleased Frank no end.

The idea that obstructions were in fact revelations also filled Frank with hope. He thought of the obstructions in his own life. He thought of the revelation that was Heide, only to realise that maybe she was an obstruction, too. He thought of the hours he had spent writing to her – how the activity had slotted into his life, as uncomplicated as a legitimate hobby, as stubborn as a young bamboo. How stupid had he been not to realise that he'd redirected all his conversation towards one person – that he'd stared so closely at the branch he'd missed the setting sun.

Frank realised how much he'd shrunk back. He peeled a Post-it note from the pad and wrote the word 'Romanticism', and next to it an arrow pointing to the word 'monasticism'. A monkish isolation was safer than a romantic one. He would fall back on that.

But then again, none of his relatives seemed to see him

either. Living under the same roof as someone, checking up on their check-ups – that didn't mean shit. That wasn't the same as a person seeing you, really seeing you. No one in this family understood him. And for all their accusations against him, none of them actually cared what he had to say. He could help with essays. He could be entrusted with anger. He could lend money. But no one ever asked. Friedrich had been misunderstood in his time, too. The best thing about Heide's letters was that they gave Frank a reason to respond. The mirror quality of his relationship with H was not lost on him.

He peeled another yellow square off the pad and wrote JOAN in the middle of it. Was Joan the pine tree in a copse, or was she the wide open sky? Had he been led to her, or had she led him to something else? The circle was dizzying. And anyhow, who could ever tell for sure where the heart stood?

*

'Did you just wolf-whistle me?'

'Yes,' said Nick. 'Your ass looks great in that skirt.'

'It's not a skirt. See? It's a two-tone dress.'

Lois pulled at the fabric to illustrate her point. Nick was lying on their bed, reading a geology book he had pulled from the shelves in Frank's office. He thought that it didn't matter what type of garment it was, as long as it made her ass look great.

'It makes your ass look like a soft, billowing pillow.'

'I found it in the basement. I bought it for New Year's. In 2000.'

'It fits perfectly.'

'Yes, well,' she said, implying 'no kids'.

Lois put on some mascara she had taken earlier from Joan's bathroom. The mascara was navy-blue and clotted, like the beach tar that stuck to their sandals in Brittany. In the bedroom across from hers, Finn and Maya had fallen asleep together after lunch. Downstairs, Cole, Frank and Gitsy were watching *The Fearless Vampire Killers* on television, and in the kitchen Joan was condensing leftovers into her leftover Tupperware in the kitchen. Simon was moping around the basement.

'Do you wanna go to the bowling alley for a drink?' asked Nick. 'We could take the dog.'

'Let's go just the two of us,' Lois replied, evening the cranberry lipstick smudge on her lips.

'Even better,' said Nick.

They walked out into the night and into the gentle snowfall. The snow crunched where they packed it down with their boots. They took the stone driveway to the shortcut through the garden of some neighbours who had also added their name to the petition. They emerged onto the small, shrub-lined road that snaked down to the main road. The windows of renovated barns and rendered houses glowed from the light and activity within.

They crossed the main road into the deserted supermarket

car park and across to the bowling alley. As they approached, they picked up the purr of the bar's blue neon sign. Lois pushed open the door. The bowling alley was bathed in a lonely white light and smelled like cooking oil. Music from the jukebox bounced off the carpeted walls, quieter than the noise of rolling balls. There was no one behind the bar. A party of four were playing on one of the alleys. Three people sat at a table, smoking and laughing. When Lois walked up to the bar, one of the men got up from the table to serve her. He continued talking to his friends from there. Lois ordered two beers and two shots of whisky, and joined Nick in the window. The bartender went back to his friends.

'Merry Christmas,' said Nick, as they downed their shots. 'Something weird happened last night,' he said, fiddling with the shot glass.

'What's that, then.'

'Tara tried to kiss me.'

'My brother's girlfriend tried to kiss you.'

'Ex. His ex-girlfriend.'

On the lanes, someone scored a strike.

'Wait,' said Lois. 'Really?'

'Yeah. It was weird.'

'What did you do?'

'Nothing. I didn't want to embarrass her.'

'So you thought you'd just *embrasse* her instead.'

'Very funny.'

'Did you kiss her?'

'No. Not really.'

'What do you mean, not really?'

'I mean, I didn't initiate or respond, but for a second her lips were on my face, so no, not really.'

After she and the Historian kissed, Lois had tried to recall who, of the Historian or her, had initiated the kiss. They were standing side by side near a metal fence, by one of the defunct piers at the end of 14th Street. The Historian was chewing gum, like he always did. He leaned into her and stopped, his minty breath hovering an inch from her mouth. She didn't move, knowing full well that in this case, immobility was an invitation.

Mentally exhuming the kiss in the bowling alley gave her a sudden headrush – an immediate, drastic yearning for that yearning of a couple of years ago, when his hand had come to rest on her hip. Warm hand, cold breath. What was she even doing standing by the water with him, on a morning in November when she should have been at home or at work, like a normal person.

'What was she even doing at the house?' she asked.

'The dog was in their garden.'

Lois drank from her glass.

'I don't need to tell you that—'

'No,' she said. 'You don't.'

'OK.'

A couple of months ago, Lois was walking down Fifth Avenue when she thought she spotted the Historian at some distance ahead of her. She trailed him for five blocks, and when he turned a corner she sprinted to catch up with him. But it wasn't him. Nor did it happen just once.

'Maybe we could go home now and have sex and you can slap my face and tell me how disappointed in me you are,' Nick ventured.

Lois took some coins out of her pocket and put them on the table. Nick followed her out of the bar. The fire door slammed shut behind them. The snow was falling much faster and thicker, a stream of tiny dry crystals that had already erased their earlier footprints. Lois thought of Tara leaning in to kiss Nick, and her mouth filled with the taste of mint.

'You're such a dog. I didn't know you were such a dog.'

She pulled out Simon's leash from her pocket.

'Here, dog. Maybe I should keep you on a tighter leash.' Lois walked over to Nick and tied Simon's leather leash around his neck gently, folding his shirt collar back over it. 'I mean, if you can't be trusted not to go snogging my brother's girlfriends.'

'Ex-girlfriend.'

'Sorry – ex-girlfriends.'

Nick was standing underneath a lamp post, the snow spiralling down the orange shaft of light and falling on his hair. Lois took his cheeks in her hands and kissed him on the lips. He tasted like nothing. Like nothing at all.

'I'll walk you home.'

Nick fell to his knees and crawled back up the road, on the frozen dirt, the icy grass cracking under his knees. Lois pulled at the leash, forcing him to hurry up.

When they reached the house, everyone had gone to bed. Simon was standing by the box of dog biscuits. They ignored him and went upstairs. Nick peeled Lois's clothes off and sniffed her skin, running his nose along her like a dog. She smelled of something, but not exactly of herself.

11. Boxing Day

THE STAR AT the top of the Christmas tree blinked erratically at Joan, like a stuttering relic from a less dysfunctional time. In four or five days, Joan would remove all the ornaments and roll them up in the yellowing kitchen towel whose job was to keep them safe for another year. Joan always took the tree down before the 30th, sometimes the 31st, not wanting the new year to land among last year's props. She considered leaving the tree put this year, relinquishing the responsibility of according their lives with the calendar. If she did, she wondered how long it would take Frank to notice. Would he mention it two weeks from now, when half the needles had fallen off, and the tips of the branches pointed to the floor under the weight of the decorations? Or would he not say a thing until February, when the branches were brittle and the tree looked like the corpse it had been for a while? Perhaps he wouldn't say anything at all, and it would be Wim who noticed, when he came home for Easter, that the Christmas tree was still up.

Joan wondered how long it would take him to notice her absence, if she left one morning. Would he miss her at lunchtime, when Simon barked for his afternoon walk, and nothing materialised on the kitchen table, or at night, when the desire to say something unimportant to furnish a silence that didn't matter would become too hard to ignore.

In the kitchen, Lois was making Nick's family recipe for clam dip. Joan poured herself a sherry and walked over to the office, Simon in tow. She looked into the piano room, where Gitsy was busy putting Calico Critters in among Joan's figurines. There was a monkey in a priest's habit, a whole cat family and a pair of unaccompanied baby panda twins.

She closed the door to the office. Simon, who preferred to move between rooms but was now stuck in there with her, lay down on the twined rug.

'I'm thinking of getting my own place,' she told him. 'Like Sue. You know – a two-bedroom apartment in one of those converted barns.'

She took a small stack of sheets out of the printer and sat down at the desk. To her left was Frank's laptop, sitting closed on top of a pile of books about German Romanticism and that service station chapbook Lois had sent them last year. To her right was the near-empty shoebox of photos. The pictures of the kids had been divvied up, and all that remained were photos of Joan seen through Frank's eyes, and vice versa.

Dear Frank, she wrote at the top of the page.

Simon's jaw yawned open and dropped a ladder of drool onto the rug. Here it was. Saint Joan's act of renunciation. He, for one, was expecting it.

*

Dear Frank,

Remember when you wrote those letters to me, the summer I went back to England? That was the summer you wrote to me every day. I remember tearing them open, and rushing to get past the 'Dear Joni' to make sure we were still one another's, and that you weren't breaking up with me because some German girl had decided to return to the Alps after all.

Those letters were the tonic of my summer. The more you missed me, the more I became obvious to myself. They were so romantic that even the postcards had to be sealed in an envelope. I try to recall what letters I sent back – how I presented myself to you back then. Or perhaps I didn't. Perhaps I was only there in your letters, and perhaps, in the same way, you found yourself in mine.

Every letter seemed to add a layer to the rubbing of me: adding more detail, making each part more obvious, perhaps a little darker.

I remember trying to intercept the letters before anyone else got to them, for fear I would come across as believing I was better than them, with my exotic boyfriend who pined for me in the French Alps. I loved the daily delivery (sometimes there were none for a few days, and then a stack of them all at once that would need to be opened chronologically, based on the postmark), but I could sense that for my family it was all pyrotechnics.

By July you promised me the future, again and again. I struggled with the idea that I was a fraud – like I must have somehow lied to you about my worth or appeal. But I kept these thoughts to myself. I still have every one of those letters somewhere. It's the one part of our marriage where the only version I held onto was yours.

I was never much of a writer.

This is the third such letter I've written to you. I tore up the other two almost immediately. The first one I wrote after the miscarriage, or as I like to remember it: the simultaneous dismissal and eviction. I felt like one of those men who leave the house every morning and then spend the rest of the day in their car, in a supermarket car park, because they can't bring themselves to tell their wives they were fired.

You, however, had somewhere else to go to process what the world doled out – a place away from us and our contract. Like an immaterial country house. That was your first retreat. Before that, I used to think of us as two yolks in one shell.

I wrote the second one two months ago, when I found out you'd been writing to an ex-girlfriend you hadn't spoken to in thirty-five years. The same one that had me scared, thirty-four years ago, that my happiness was at her whim. What got to me wasn't even the writing (and yes, I read your correspondence), it was something you said about regret.

I never wanted to be part of anyone's regret, Frank.

For thirty-five years I've watched you exercise your power of choice. Over the years you've chosen your clients, where you go for lunch, if and when you'll join me and the kids on holiday. Jobs, structural changes to the house, what to obsess over, how much time to devote to dead German painters, if and when to pay our taxes. Who to declare undying devotion to, who to include in your pre-twilight regrets.

It is true there are some things I got to choose. New shoes for the kids, summer camps, what to make for dinner, which time slot for the parent-teacher conference… And you. I chose you.

Writing to you today, I am aware it isn't just about a German woman who never had your children. I am opening a vent on the exhaustion I can and have contained for years. It exhausts me to watch you exist so far away from us. These days, if I want to share something with you, I am put off by the sheer distance between us. For years now you've been living in a 'bor' of your own making: an ill-defined grotto no one really cares about that doesn't even exist in reality. You can't see that all this is the symptom of a family man who has taken a giant step out of the circle, and is unable to name the place he's chosen to hide out in.

For a long time I felt stupid that I was content with what was obviously so lacking for you. I felt like I had what I needed, and wanted, in you, the children. I made your bunker cosy, I watched the children while you moved into your parallel universe. I fought alongside you, but it was always your kingdom.

It's not that you don't need me – I can see that you do. But you need me like you need an anchor. I don't want to be an anchor. I want to be lighter than that.

You are as in love as you are obsessed. You pore over paintings of man as a speck in mountain majesty. You stare at invisible swamps and holes in the ground, as if they were part of your reality. And today you've become one of the observers you study. You've become a thesis in dissociation.

We are the wings of the diorama, Frank. You've always felt alone with us, and you think you're together with ghosts. You're winding your heart up over some woman in Hamburg, and you're not getting a check-up on the heart we need down here, in the real world.

You are scratching at the surface of the surface of another planet, Frank.

I will start looking for a place after the children leave. I want a small place, higher up in the mountains. Because, as it turns out, I love the mountains as much as you do. I never knew that. I'm going to find a better view of these mountains, Frank, and it will be my view.

Joan/Joni

Joan folded the letter and placed it inside an envelope. She took the envelope to the star-studded cupboard and slid it in between the boxes of unsorted photos. There. She was one step closer to something. She had gone and created the exit button.

*

All the Christmas leftovers in Tara's fridge were cling-filmed. There even seemed to be a dedicated shelf – jars with fuzzy green crowns, or on other containers of even older leftovers. William could see the chaos house lit up through the bamboo hedge – too many yellow glows, too many rooms empty but burning up energy. He could smell the warmth and mess from here. The only lights that were on in Tara's house were the kitchen lights and the bedside lamp in her bedroom.

Wim pulled at a tag that was scratching inside his new Christmas sweater. Tara was zapping plates of thinly sliced boeuf-en-croûte and roasted potatoes in the microwave.

'Do you want something to drink?' she asked.

'Do you have Orangina?'

There had always been Orangina in Tara's house. Also, the sideboard was never messy, and the opened bills were filed there in a manageable and not unattractive pile. The maelstrom in his parents' house was never far away. It was expertly hidden by Joan, but it was there. Like the dresser in the dining room. On top of it sat the two pine-green, hand-painted candelabra that had been Joan's first real adult purchase. But if you opened the top three drawers, you found unopened bills going back ten years. And three bottom rows of drawers were full of VHS tapes – many of them in the wrong boxes. There wasn't even a VCR in the house, just hundreds of VHS tapes.

The microwave pinged, and Tara took out the reheated leftovers using a pot holder she'd made in Year Eight. Wim remembered making a pot holder too, that year. Watching Tara scrape the bottom of the mustard jar with a knife, he was overcome with the desire to kiss her. The kiss made Tara drop the knife, which left a grainy yellow streak on the brown tiles. He tried to kiss Tara again as she bent down to pick it up.

'Get off,' she yelled, pushing him away. 'What's your fucking problem?'

It made no sense to be in this kitchen, at this table, in this too-blue sweater, so close to Tara and about to eat roast beef.

'I'm sorry.'

'What is your fucking problem?' she repeated, appearing to want an answer.

Wim took the sponge from the sink and cleaned the mustard off the floor.

'Shall I get out of here?' asked Wim.

'Can't we just fucking sit down and eat? Can you just sit down?'

Wim grabbed the Orangina that Tara had put on the table and poured himself a glass.

'You're all over the place,' said Tara, who clearly wasn't.

He cut into the meat, which seeped pale blood onto the plate. If they could still be friends, eating leftovers, if he didn't fuck it up, again, maybe they could be like divorced adults. He wondered if it was too late for Joan and Frank to become divorced adults. If they had missed the boat on that one.

'When do you have to go back?' asked Tara.

'I have to be back by the third.'

The next few days were for turning the page.

'You wanna drive to Italy?' she asked. 'I have the car, and my parents are at my aunt's for the next few days anyway.'

Yes, he did want to drive to Italy. He hadn't seen Lois in months, and he knew Joan would be upset. But they would understand. Maya and the kids were leaving tomorrow anyway. Frank had given him 300 euros this morning. They could stay in a cheap hotel. Eat osso buco and bring back cans of vongole for Joan. He could pay for everything. Tara could take charge of where to go and what to do.

'All right,' he said, bringing his plate to the sink.

'Go get your stuff, then,' she said. 'Let's just go.'

He didn't need anything. In that moment, it felt like he had everything he needed right there.

*

Gitsy was busy applying the new cherry-scented nail polish to her toes when Lois walked into the room with the phone.

Maya was filling a see-through plastic box with the clothes that Finn and Gitsy had almost outgrown. She tore off a piece of masking tape and labelled the box. 'Kids' clothes/Maya'. Even though she was the only one with kids.

'It's Liz for you,' said Lois, handing the phone to Maya.

'Very funny,' said Maya.

'She says that's very funny,' Lois said into the receiver.

'Who's Liz?' asked Gitsy.

She put the nail polish wand down onto the green carpet, which was already spattered with little flecks of fuchsia.

Maya snatched the phone from Lois's hand.

'Hello?'

'Who's Liz?' Gitsy asked again.

'Wait one sec,' said Maya. 'I'm going downstairs.'

Maya ran down to the basement with the phone. Simon managed to slink through the useless door before she slammed it shut.

'I've been calling your phone,' said Liz.

Liz's voice calmed Maya down instantly. Liz sounded completely normal, as though the order of their relationship was unchanged.

'I threw my phone into a field a couple of nights ago.'

'Seems reasonable enough.'

Maya walked over to the corner of the biggest room in the basement. A leak from the first floor had formed a small puddle on the polished concrete and left a tea-coloured cloud on the ceiling. Maya placed the leak somewhere near the crèche, in the pianoless room.

'What's up?'

'Not much,' said Maya. 'They're all driving me crazy. I miss you.'

'I miss you too.'

'Mum?' Gitsy called through the door. Maya stood still and muffled the receiver with her hand. 'Mama?' After a while, Gitsy stopped calling.

'Are you still there?'

'Yes,' said Maya. 'There's something weird going on between my sister and the dog.'

'What do you mean, weird?'

She wasn't sure what she meant. Just that Lois, like her parents, had suddenly become a dog person. It sounded crazy, but Lois seemed to favour the dog over her niece and nephew.

'She could at least take them out to make a snowman.'

'I'm not following,' said Liz.

Maya thought she heard a splash in the background. She looked through the French windows, which connected the underused basement to the garden and hadn't been washed in years. Beyond the window was the pool, covered by a fine sheet of ice. The whole garden was a deathtrap, thought Maya.

'How's your colleague?' she asked.

'I'm not sleeping with her if that's the question.'

'I'm not sure I believe you.'

Simon started to lap up the water that had pooled on the floor. Maya gave him a gentle kick to move him away from the puddle. He looked up at her with indignant eyes.

'I think when we get back you should leave your husband.'

'OK.'

'I'm not sure I believe you.'

Simon walked over to the other side of the room and lay down next to his old crate.

'Tell me the truth,' said Liz. 'Is that even on your radar?'

'There's no such thing as truth,' said Maya. 'Only present and future decisions.'

'Mama?'

Gitsy's little voice came up from the dark corner of the basement like a wisp of clear air.

'I have to go.'

Maya hung up and followed the corridor round to the room that Frank had originally intended as a wine cellar. Gitsy was sitting on the floor looking up at the ceiling. Her night-sky projector was plugged into the wall, and throwing up spiralling constellations onto the unfinished concrete surfaces.

Maya walked over and put her hand against her daughter's hot cheek.

'Is it the dark times, Mama?'

The words came out of Gitsy's mouth like tin soldiers, and came to point their muskets at Maya's face. Maya saw how the light in her own world was being sucked out of Gitsy's peace, drop by drop, and how her feelings for Liz were an oil slick waiting to happen in Gitsy's heart.

Gitsy was too young for the dark times. Maya remembered the dark times as having landed when she was eight. She could remember the exact moment. She and Lois were playing upstairs with their dolls' house. There was a light switch on the outside wall that turned the lights on and off inside. The tiny bulbs all went on and off at the same time, like a power outage. Joan, who had been making reassuring sounds in the kitchen, suddenly went quiet. The silence coaxed both Maya and Lois away from the dolls' house and onto the mezzanine. Joan was still in the kitchen, talking in hushed tones to someone on the phone. Every now and again she whispered, 'No!' and then, 'I'm sorry. I am so, so sorry.'

Later that night, the girls spied on Joan and Frank and found out that a friend of Joan's had just lost her sister. Her sister had jumped out of a window. The dark times had slipped into Maya and Lois like a curse, punishing them for eavesdropping. They had grown progressively darker, until that light of no fear was no longer even distant but altogether gone, a thing from another time.

'Is it the dark times, Mama?' Gitsy insisted.

'The dark times?'

'Yes. I mean, is it dark outside?'

'Oh.'

Perhaps Gitsy could be spared for a few more years. 'Not yet, darling. It's just very dark in the basement. Let's go upstairs and find the others.'

Gitsy wrapped her fingers around Maya's hand, locking her there, away from the phone, which connected back to Liz, who also needed her. Maya was trapped in Gitsy's goodness, Gitsy's love of their unit, and as she felt the squeeze of her daughter's paw every time her hand grew lax, she cared less and less about the phone call, and about the things Liz might be saying, or thinking, or asking for, had she not hung up.

*

That night, Lois found Frank's Christmas gift on her pillow. He must have put it there just before leaving for the airport to drop off Nick. It lay on the pillow like an afterthought, crudely wrapped in paper retrieved from the recycling. It was book-shaped. Each one of those three facts was as predictable as the other.

This was the order of things. Frank observed, watched his family expiate their little rituals from afar, but eventually he chimed in. Is that what it was? Or was it just that he was always won over by the spirit a bit too late? The idea that she might have misread her father for thirty-two years was too daunting for Lois to grapple with, so she let it rest.

Inside the package, which was held together with the masking tape Joan used to label things, anything, were three old notebooks. The binding on the notebooks was faded and coming apart at the corners. The first notebook was filled with writing that was trembly and dense, like a child's handwriting in an old person's notebook. Little grey words filled the page and margins. The letters were long and spindly, like fly legs.

Lois opened the notebook to the first page. At the very top, a date: Argenteuil, 1951. Below the date, in the middle of the line, a name: Maria Acerbo. Below that, a title: 'A Remarkable Moment in Our History'. The History in question started just underneath, without so much as a line break from the title's promise.

It was when I was five that Mother put us on a boat to Villa San Giovanni, and then on trains to France. It took forever to leave Italy, and until we had crossed the border we thought she might still change her mind, and abandon this plan that made sense only in an abstract, adult way. Which is to say no sense at all to us. My brother didn't speak a word the whole way. Benedetta and Rosamaria were giddy with excitement, and spent most of the journey doing and undoing each other's hair so they could practise fashionable hairstyles. Mother, who usually would have scolded such vanity, stared out of the window the whole time.

I wish I could remember the sight of Italy growing more distant through the window, but all I can remember is her furrowed, sad brow, and her eyes that seemed to say don't ask anything of me now. We spent two nights in Turin, all six of us in a hotel room. It was the first time we had stayed in a hotel room, but it didn't feel glamorous. The room was small and smelly, and there was no light. There was a sink at the end of the corridor, where we and everyone else on the floor had to wash. In the end we spent two nights there. I don't know if she had planned it that way, or if Mother was afraid of the final leg of the trip, like she still might change her mind. In any case, we stayed in Italy one more night, knowing that the next day we would hold hands as the train went across the border and that there would be no turning back.

I spent my first day in France on a train, eating bread. Benedetta and Rosamaria were pretending to speak French and putting on airs and steaming up the train window, and then kissing it to see the mark their lips left there. They had a kissing competition. Each thought she was the winner. The colours were different in France. The roofs were dark-brown, and the trees not scorched. I remember the farms looked particularly different. The towns we stopped at seemed huge to me, and terrifying. I can't remember the names of those towns now. The people looked cold – as in chilly – and not particularly happy. No one spoke to us the whole journey. When we got out in Paris, Mother made us hold hands so we wouldn't get lost. As we walked through the station like a long snake, I was concerned that if I got lost here I would never see anyone I loved ever again.

We left Mariella back in Salice, in the cemetery. We covered her with flowers the day before we left, like people who leave food out for the dog when they leave for days. I didn't want to live in a different country from my favourite sister.

The reason we moved is that Father stopped sending money. Mother wrote to him, and when he didn't answer she wrote to his brother's wife, and then to his brother, who were also in France. No one wrote back, and there wasn't enough for all the children with the money Mother made in the fields. Mother told her sister that my father must have another woman in Paris. My sisters overheard them talking about the other woman in Paris and played at being her.

In the end, we never saw another woman. Mother purchased some land from an Italian mason who came from the same village as her parents, and we all helped make the bricks. We slept at our aunt and uncle's house for three months while we built ours. When the house was finished is when we went to find Father. Not before. Mother went to find him in a bar where she'd heard he bet on the horse races. She dragged him out by the scruff of the neck and marched him to the new house with us kids following behind, and no one ever spoke another word about it.

*

'Hopi art', from *The Yelp Travel Plaza Review Poetry* Log, by Lois
Lemaire (Incomprehensible Womb Press, 2014)

eastbound for Hopi art we fuel here
(we, six adults and three children)
fountain drinks to hot-air hand dryer

you've got your dining options out rear
and your nickel discount per gallon
eastbound for Hopi art we fuel here

McDonalds, Honey Dew Donuts, we're
giving high praise: the restrooms are clean
fountain drinks to hot-air hand dryer

must-stop joe, they shuttered the diner
mirrors missing from the pavilion
eastbound for Hopi art we fuel here

condiments free, friendly cashier,
save our spinach for this number one
fountain drinks to hot-air hand dryer

modern remodel, nice souvenir
there was no salt but the dog had fun

eastbound for Hopi art we fuel here
fountain drinks to hot-air hand dryer

Cole closed the chapbook and put it back on the shelf. Definitely an oddball, that one, he thought. In the kitchen, the dog was licking up the crumbs that had been swept off the counter.

12. Historical Monument

THE CITY BENEATH him looked like a circuit board. The familiar electricity of its avenues and motorways was turned on for his landing, welcoming him home. All those windows and lives and pilot lights. All those beating hearts and distinct wills. He thought of the cleaners, sopping up the hallways of office buildings on streets that would keep on dwarfing them till they died. Of the security guards and doormen who worked the graveyard shift, and watched over the city's down hours. He thought of those who still took baths in their kitchen. Like that girl he'd dated briefly, before he met Lois. She had a spot on Tomkins Square Park, with a corner window and a huge chopping board under which the bathtub vanished in the day. He imagined the men who would soon be inside their street-corner fortresses, selling coffee and egg sandwiches near the city's building sites. And then he thought of Lois, fast asleep and dissatisfied, grinding her teeth under her mother's quilt.

He was happy to be home. Away from those crazy, self-obsessed French people who finished each others' sentences but couldn't tell the truth.

Before he left, Frank had given him one of his purple mountain crystals. It was a stone he'd prized off the mountain as a young man, when the mountains were still a thing to be conquered. When Frank was not yet an old man getting lost in the hills behind his house.

The gift of the crystal came out of left field. It wasn't the culmination of a conversation about rocks, or even geology, or youth, or anything. Frank just appeared with the rock and handed it to Nick. Nick took it as Frank's way of belatedly sealing their relationship, of acknowledging – not without relief – at least one shared interest with his son-in-law.

On his last night in France, Frank had shown him pictures of a recent chalet renovation. Old beams and lots of glass, a neat mineral-grey infinity pool overlooking doll-sized valleys – wealth that got stashed away in barn conversions and altitude.

He wondered how Joan could bear it. How she could still, after thirty-five years, run her errands in this rarefied town, which changed so slowly that whatever change did occur got lost in time. And how could she bear living with Frank, who seemed less and less able to empathise with anything that didn't relate directly to him, these days.

He worried about Joan. He worried about Joan in the same way he worried about himself. He saw Frank's isolation drag her down, harden her. You could no longer ask Joan how she was doing and give any credence to her answer. Lois often told him she thought Joan should leave Frank. She and Maya said that now – now that they had flown the coop, now that the impact of their parents' separation on their own lives would be minimal. They hadn't always thought that way.

On the subway home, he imagined a conversation in which Lois said she wouldn't be coming back. Then he imagined a conversation in which she came home, but it was he who asked her to find somewhere else to live. He also imagined himself repainting the kitchen to surprise her, and leaving white carnations in a vase on the table for when she arrived. He couldn't tell if this Christmas was to be racked up with the good ones or not. He had felt close to Lois, yes, but that could have been familiarity. Seeing Lois and Frank together had sobered him. Lois sometimes joked that she'd grow into her mum, but what if she grew into her dad?

He still didn't know if she'd told Frank and Joan about her affair. He hoped not. The way they were so protective of her, and tolerant – it would have angered him to think they knew and hadn't given her hell. Hadn't submitted her to the adult version of a grounding. Reminded her that even unconditional love is a deal, that they were all married to Nick, in a way. He'd not told his parents. 'I don't want them to think any less of you,' he told Lois. The truth is, he was scared it made him look like a sap.

Was he a sap?

People got on and off the subway. Perhaps they knew a thing or two about rocks. Perhaps they didn't. All these strangers were like geodes – crystallised around bubbling emotions that left their core unfilled.

When he got home he opened his suitcase and found a draft of Lois's lovelords manuscript. There was a Post-it note on it that said, 'I love you'. He poured himself a whisky and sat on the bed. He opened it to the first page. It was dedicated to Frank.

Still, it was only love.

*

'Like dogs', from *A Battleground Is Love*, by Lois Lemaire (Incomprehensible Womb Press, t.b.a.)

I am 9
I am 14
I am 17, 18 and 22
I am 33
they treat us like dogs
like less than dogs
like volunteers and
can I have 5 minutes
to hold

you
close?
you've asked me, like,
6 times
yes, but
if I had asked
for 30 minutes
you would have
said
no.

*

'Let's go to the Monument,' Joan said at breakfast. Maya, Cole and the kids were flying back to DC tomorrow. The snow from last night had set into a thick white coat that elevated everything several feet up from the ground. Lois was cutting and pasting words on her laptop, and Frank was ensconced in the hefty dictionary of ancient geography he'd left under the tree for himself. He didn't know what to do with himself in the wake of the latest interdiction – this one doled out to preserve not his, but Joan's heart. Joan suspected that if she could only get them walking in the snow and expending energy, by this evening they would all be too tired to be themselves, and to have any arguments.

After breakfast, Maya helped Joan rummage through the boxes in the hall closet for old hats and gloves. The kids' gloves had stayed un-lost at the end of elastic that had long lost its bounce. The children sometimes used them as skipping ropes or weapons. Lois filled all the thermoses she could find with tea, except for one, which she filled with instant hot chocolate for Gitsy. Frank put his fat book and a handful of dog treats together in a plastic bag.

Joan, Cole and the kids piled into the rental car. Frank, Maya and Lois got into Frank's garbage car. Simon lay down in the boot, on top of the gloves and hats. On the drive to the Monument, Lois and Maya resuscitated the memory of a meteor shower they had observed there one year. There were fireballs in the sky that night, and orange embers in the stony pit at their feet. Lois had more or less ruined the night by prodding Maya's hair with a melted marshmallow. That was the thing about bad behaviour – it ruined the moment but made for a better memory. Frank looked at Lois in the rear-view mirror and wondered if Joan had finally said something about H. He felt sure Joan had told Maya, although it was unlike Maya not to say anything.

In the car park, Gitsy ran over to Frank's car. 'Daddy said that Grandpa made the toilet. It's open, you can even go inside.'

Frank had won the commission almost thirty years ago. It had been his first public contract. He went on to design more public amenities – starting with rotaries and bus shelters, and working his way up to low-income housing and the municipal conservatory. The public toilet was one of the more stressful assignments he'd ever had to deliver. To come up with a space that was discreet yet functional, and was somehow in conversation with the values underpinning a monument to fallen war heroes. The monument, a V-shaped symbol made of poured concrete, towered over the forest to be remembered.

As she rummaged around in the boot for the children's hats and gloves and scarves, Maya spied Frank trying to slip his fingers through Joan's, and Joan retracting her hand.

Cole was explaining to Gitsy that during World War Two, men had hidden up in this forest to fight.

'Are there still men fighting in the forest?' asked Gitsy. A couple of cross-country skiers emerged from the trees and glided into the white clearing.

'No,' said Cole.

'Did they use Grandpa's toilet?' she asked. Trapped in the Baby Björn, Finn was nodding off against Cole's chest, oblivious to anything but his warm suspension.

Lois thought of the men in the woods, afraid to die and even more afraid of life as it was panning out. She thought of the dead boy in the video. She wondered what the boy's mother was doing at this exact moment in time. Was she hanging out clothes on a washing line, thinking of her dead son? Was she lying on her bed, convulsed with grief, still, because her eyes had perhaps stopped on a picture of him graduating high school?

What Lois was doing – all the snipping, the collaging – suddenly seemed futile. The words had meant something, once. Words that came through a radio, words that were carried by hand through a valley and up a cliff, words that had informed one person of the arrival of troops, another of a humanitarian convoy. Her de-naturing was pointless, pretentious. The love poems existed for no one but her. She had no lovers, she would have no readers. The project was just another file that got saved and opened and closed like a front door by the wind.

She would call Nick, tell him not to bother reading it. Tell him it needed another pass. Tell him the last thing it needed was her touch. The last thing he needed was her touch. He still hadn't called.

Real truth came from the silences. From the lack of words. Simon rolled in the snow at her feet and she squatted down to reach his belly. There were no questions between her and Simon. There was no intimacy and yet there were intimations that got solved by a walk, a scratch, or a bowl of food. There was no need to sustain and even less need to create. In fact, there was no need at all – just a mutual, needless assistance.

They followed a trail up to the ledge where they had once watched a celestial shower. Snow covered the grassy platform they remembered, and the flat rocks they'd once sat on revealed only a few inches of themselves today. Gitsy started to pile up snow at the adults' feet. Soon the pile looked like a snowy sausage link.

'What is it?' asked Frank.

'It's your sleeping lady,' she said.

Joan took a mouthful of tea from the thermos and spat it out in the snow.

'What's wrong?' asked Maya.

'Someone put salt in the tea instead of sugar.'

*

Frank walked into the café and took his usual table by the window. He watched the cars zoom past in the early morning, to the sound of the coffee machine and the clink of euro centimes on the counter. He opened the paper and stared into it like a view. The waitress brought over his espresso and made the customary enquiries about Christmas and family, to which Frank gave the customary answers about health and luck.

Under the table, Simon licked up the lost crumbs from a croissant and wondered whether Lois would take him for a walk that afternoon, and if so, where they would go. To the kayak dock, he hoped. Yesterday, at the monument, Simon had struggled in the snow. Eventually he evicted Gitsy from the sled and Frank dragged him back to the car. Gitsy had a giant snow-angel tantrum, and wouldn't stop until Lois gave her a piggyback.

Frank found nothing he wanted to read in the paper this morning and folded it back up. He drank up and brought the empty coffee cup to the bar. 'Can I buy a scratch card?' he asked, dropping coins onto the bar.

'Which one?'

'I don't know the difference.'

'Well, I sometimes get this one. I've won two euros before.'

'Ok, I'll take ten of those.'

'Why don't you do one of each? You don't want to put all your eggs in one basket.'

'No,' said Frank. 'I don't.'

The bartender put the scratch cards in one of the little paper bags they used for postcards and handed it to Frank. He would give them to Joan. A late Christmas present. Maybe she would win the lottery. Maybe she would be happy again with him, then.

At home he sat in his office and opened up the computer. There was an email from one of his clients with questions about the counter top for a kitchen island and an issue with the wet room. 'Bathroom,' he said out loud. 'It's a bathroom, for God's sake.' He answered the client and unblocked Heide. He blocked her again. He did this several times, clicking and unclicking. It was as simple as that. In. Out. In. Out. Having someone in your life or not was just a click of a finger.

Frank took a large sheet of paper and went down to the dining room. He taped the paper to the table and drew a jaggy mountain at the top of the page. He drew another hill in the foreground and populated it with a cluster of A-frame chalets. He added a stream and a footpath. At the top of the first mountain he pencilled in a tiny refuge.

'Gitsy, do you want to draw with me?'

Gitsy came over to the table and sat down next to Frank. He pushed the box of coloured pencils in her direction and instructed her to add some bloom to the meadows. Gitsy ignored this, instead tracing a string of curlicues along the edge of the page. Maya observed this interaction from the kitchen.

'Why did they build it so close to the cliff?' asked Gitsy, pointing to the chalet.

'Well, they were on the edge of the world,' replied Frank.

'Where's the edge of the world?'

'It's just before the end.'

Gitsy pointed to the paper envelope on the table.

'What's that?' she asked.

'Scratch cards. You scratch them and sometimes you win a million euros.'

'Can I scratch one?'

'Sure.'

Gitsy found a coin and furiously scraped the silver carbon coating off each of the ten cards. She revealed numbers, dozens of them, fat with zeros. 'I won a million dollars!' she cried, running to show her mum the scratch cards. Frank continued to colour in the path, and to imagine a world beyond the one that was already there on the page.

13. In Love and War

IT WAS THE last day of battle. One more day to attack before he could put this strange year to rest. There were still a few offensives left to squeeze out of his troops. What was a new year if not a change of strategy? Frank had on his warsuit, the frayed bathrobe Lois had given him over a decade ago. He should have euthanized it years ago, but its familiar softness every morning was the bridge into the day, with all its setbacks and rationing. Maybe he would get rid of the bathrobe today. Buy a new one. A new bathrobe for a new year.

Maya and family had left for the airport earlier that morning. Lois was still here and was now talking of accompanying William back to London for a few days. He had called last night from Asti to say he'd be home that evening.

In a couple more days it would be Thursday, thought Frank, who was missing his heart.

Frank looked down on men who needed routine, or didn't know any better than to appreciate the same things day in day out. And yet, the change he embraced intellectually he found tedious in practice. He saw himself getting into his dirty car with the dog and the laptop, driving to Josée's and sitting down at his usual spot. He hoped they hadn't changed the menu.

Yes, he'd enjoyed seeing the kids, but he'd be happy once things got back to normal. The most annoying thing about the holiday had been losing Simon's walks to the others. The children had co-opted his habit, particularly Lois, who turned into a dog lover overnight. He saw how the others, like Maya, used Simon as a get-out-of-jail card – to escape the house and its leaden warmth and reliable web of interactions. Simon had caught on to the transaction and parcelled out his affection like capital. Still, Frank knew that once the children left, once Joan had spent all the cheer the kids had given her, Simon would come trotting back to him, because he'd be the only one left. Being a dog in the world was a bit like being stranded on a desert island with just the one other person.

The house was quiet, and since no one was up to judge, Frank went to his office and opened his laptop. He'd stayed up late last night and published the latest instalment of his CDF blog – the one about Joan and the branches. Seventeen people had liked it. One of them was Heide, who had commented a lone 'schön' under the alias Lorelei59. He had omitted to block her in the comments section. He did so now. As he looked at the computer screen and the standard template he'd customised all those months ago, his gaze pierced right through the hardware, into the abyss.

He saw Joan, in the future, in an apartment inside a converted barn that cost under a million because it was in the shade of the lying lady. He saw his own house crumbling. Slowly at first, a piece of stone architrave here, a tile there, until hairline cracks snaked down the wall and dug deep trenches under the foundations. He saw himself, several Christmases from now, in the same tattered bathrobe. He knew it was a Christmas vision because he was painfully aware of the absence of all things Christmas. He saw future Christmases without the Nativity scene. Without a poinsettia. He knew the children came home for those things. For the garden-themed ornaments fastened to the tree with brown twine, for the turkey or capon or whatever the hell it was, for the mince pies. They wouldn't come for him.

He clicked his way back to the dashboard and took his blog offline. But the vision remained, glued to the back of his eyes like a motivational poster. Joan in the future was exactly like Joan now, only without him. Joan would take the Nativity scene and the ornaments from Bavaria. He saw oysters, and someone else shucking them.

Frank looked down at his fist and saw that it was clenched. He tried to open it, to extend his fingers and unwhiten his knuckles, but he couldn't. It occurred to him that he was perhaps holding something vital in the centre of it, and that if he opened his hand that something might shoot out and lose itself in the room, in the world. As long as his fist was clenched, he kept whatever it was contained, in his body, in his arm, shooting up and down and banging up against the nerves to be let out.

He could hear his heart beating, only he couldn't be sure it was his heart. It could just as well have an invisible arrow, bouncing through his arm from palm to chest. Whatever it was, it was loud, like a generator.

Frank fell to his knees, still clenching his fist. The frayed bathrobe, barely there in places, felt like a straitjacket.

He crawled with difficulty from the desk to Simon's cushion, carrying that great lump of tightness at the end of his hand. He lay down on the bed, which smelled like wet dog, but also like braised heart. He thought he could hear Lois in the kitchen, but it could have been the television. They'd been invited to their friends' house tonight. He didn't want to go. Maybe now he could get out of it. Now what. Now what, Frank? What exactly was going on that might constitute an acceptable excuse to skip an invitation negotiated by Joan?

Frank looked up at the ceiling. His arm, limp on the bed, felt as if it were pinned to a corkboard with a dagger.

It was the last day of the battle.

Frank looked up at the ceiling and thought of his heart. His tiny, old-man, purple, diseased heart. He thought of his heart and how it always came with a garnish of lambs' lettuce.

*

From the window by Frank's hospital bed, Joan could see the mountain they sometimes climbed with the kids, back when they were young and starting out, and lived in the apartment in the old town. From this angle, the mountain looked like a dark-green jaw with five grey teeth pointing upwards. They had scaled it with the children from the side, up a gentle path most of the way. The last hour was a steep climb, and there was a via ferrata in the rocks to help with the ascent. At the top of the mountain was a snack bar that opened in late spring and stayed open until October. It sold sodas, sandwiches and souvenirs. They used to go there. They used to go to Italy for the weekend. Stock up on tins of clams and medlars. Sleep in hotel rooms and leave the beds unmade in the morning. But somewhere down the line, Frank had taken those hours and days and weekends and given them over to his stupid maps. He'd spent so much time searching for 'bors', he'd become one himself.

Frank's eyes opened. The first thing he noticed was the white poinsettia Joan had put on the bedside table. It was one of the two poinsettias from the living-room coffee table. The second thing he noticed was that Joan had opened the blinds.

In the cold-day sunlight she looked much younger, had an almost holy glow. Joan was looking out at the other side of the lake, the side where they should have bought the land for the house, all those years ago. Back in the time of possibility.

'What did you think would happen, Frank?'

'I don't know,' he said. 'Nothing.'

Next door a machine started beeping, slowly at first, and then faster and faster.

'I didn't think beyond just writing,' said Frank.

'No, you idiot. What did you think would happen if you kept eating meat and salt?'

'Oh.'

She had come looking for him. When she opened the door to the study, he was lying on the dog's bed with his eyes closed. She said his name, several times, and asked him a question. He couldn't remember what the question was, only that he was unable to answer, busy as he was breathing through the pain in his chest. He had known with great certainty, in that moment, that if he should open his mouth to answer Joan, all the breaths left in his body would come flying out and escape through that five-inch gap under the cellar door.

Everything after that was vague. He remembered the ambulance, and the ambulance man, who reminded him of his client in Dubai. Perhaps they were driving him to a site meeting, or to pick out some tiles. There was more shifting of his body through unknown spaces, and then sleep. He wasn't sure how long he'd been lying in this hospital bed. The clock on the wall said 1.40 p.m. He'd woken up earlier and a doctor with a clipboard had spoken to him. He'd woken up again some hours later when the nurse brought his lunch on a plastic tray. Everything on the plate was the same wheat-paste shade: mashed potato, cauliflower, chicken in a white sauce. He hadn't touched it.

He'd promised to go look at that wet room. It seemed unlikely he would get round to it today. He would give the client a call, later. He thought of Simon, at home, standing by his box of biscuits. Would Lois remember to feed him? Walk him? He wondered what the dog had done when they'd taken him off in the ambulance. Had he barked? Had he followed him to the ambulance, whimpering, and did he howl as it disappeared down the driveway? You heard of some dogs that never got over their master's death. Would Simon curl up in the bamboos and die if he didn't make it out of hospital? Isn't that what dogs were wired to do?

Frank uncurled his fingers in Joan's direction. She took his hand and rested it on his chest, hers on top of it. He could feel something thumping through the closed knot of their two hands.

'Have you spoken to the cardiologist yet?' asked Joan.

'I think it was him I saw this morning.'

'What did he say?'

'That it was only a mild heart attack,' said Frank.

'So they found a heart.'

Earlier she had moved the letter to Frank from the starry cupboard to her sock drawer.

To be lying in a hospital bed with Joan at his side was all right, thought Frank. It would be awful to be debilitated around someone like H. Someone you only knew from when you were young, when your body was still a firm ally, one that didn't need to be factored into everything. Joan had nursed their children back to health through tummy aches, ear infections, broken toes and arms, the flu. She was a steady hand. She couldn't help but be devoted. Wired that way.

'What would you do,' Frank asked Joan, 'if you found out you had only one year left to live?'

'The bigger question is, what would I do if I had many more years left to live?'

She thought she might want to run her own business. That was one of them. She didn't know what kind of business she wanted to run, just that she, too, wanted to make decisions every day that were of minor consequence to people she knew less well than her relatives. She wanted to be told she was stunning. Wanted to extract a few more gasps, even if it was from her husband. She wanted, twenty-two years too late, to rest her head on a shoulder and cry about the miscarriage, about her mother. She wanted to move to where her daughters were. She wanted to move to Brittany, where her daughters weren't. She never said any of those things out loud because, with time, Frank had become a kind of a receptacle where information came to be abandoned – like foreign coins in the key bowl.

As she got ready to leave for the hospital earlier that day, Joan's eyes stopped on the picture of Frank on the fridge door. The memory came flooding back. It was she who had taken the picture. It didn't predate her. Didn't belong to a history that was only hers by proxy. It wouldn't need to be carbon-dated after all. The clue was the wine bottle in the bottom-left corner of the picture, on the picnic blanket. They'd bought a case of them from a winery in the Piedmont. Weeks after the trip, they'd carried one of the bottles up the sleeping lady, for a picnic. Later that day they'd come upon a tiny lake – a shallow, chalky turquoise puddle that hovered over grey stones.

Joan took her hand out of Frank's useless clasp and went to fetch the day's paper from her handbag. It was rolled around one of the gigantic bars of Toblerone they sold in the hospital gift shop.

'Lois said she'd come over in a bit.'

'Oh.'

'And one of our daughters is pregnant.'

'Oh.'

There was strictly no point in trying to keep up with those kids, thought Frank. Things changed so quickly.

Joan had spotted the test while emptying the rubbish bin

in the upstairs bathroom. The test had been slipped back into its foil pouch. At first, she hesitated over whether to look or not. The line was faint. It could have been an evaporation line – like a salt lick on a seaside rock.

'What are we going to do?' asked Joan.

'About the baby?' said Frank.

'No. About the rest of our lives?'

That was the thing about Joan, you could never tell if she was being fatalistic or utterly adventurous.

'You hold me back,' thought Frank.

Joan looked out of the window to the other side of the lake, with its shrubbed-in lawns, Michelin-star restaurant and privatised waterfront.

'You hold me back from the cliff face.'

*

Nick made a pile of his books on the coffee table. The ones from Lois had inscriptions inside them, and dates that bound them to the unrelated story of a moment in time. Above the fireplace was a framed plate of a dodo that had once hung in his childhood bedroom. He took it down and put it with the books. There was nothing else he wanted. The ashtray in the shape of a starfish, perhaps. The pen in the shape of a crab claw. The paperweight fossil. The things masquerading as others, he would take. And from the kitchen, the wooden spice rack his father had made for his mother.

All of his things fitted into two suitcases and four moving-boxes. After he loaded the Jeep with his stuff, Nick went to the hardware store and bought a new tilt latch for the bathroom window. It took him five minutes to fit it. The window slid up like it ought to, letting new air into the bathroom for the first time in two years.

Nick thought of all the little mends waiting to be performed in Frank's house. He wondered if Frank's reluctance to finish the house was perhaps deliberate. After all, once a thing was done, it could no longer be promising. And what was a relationship if not a to-do list? It was the room for amelioration that kept it (like the bathroom) airtight.

What was left to do with Lois. They'd built and obliterated, tried and failed, made and lost, come and gone. Perhaps fixing the bathroom window was the last remaining thing on their list.

Nick stood in the open window and called his mother. A giant rat scampered across the neighbours' concrete yard and disappeared under the shed. When no one picked up, he left a message to say he was driving home for New Year's.

He pulled the window down, leaving a one-inch crack to keep the apartment oxygenated for when Lois got back.

The last thing he did was tear the warning sign off the window.

*

The taxidermy blowfish was still in the window of the fishing-gear and tackle shop across from Frank's office. Its brown spikes had paled in two decades of sunlight. It had lost one of its glass eyes, but still had its bloated, whistling lips the kids imitated when they walked to Frank's office after school. William unlocked the door and let himself in.

On the left was the reception desk cubicle, with its sliding door and supply closet. William opened all the drawers, as he had as a child, to steal paperclips and still-packaged highlighters, and the staples he pushed into the wall. The drawers were empty, but the secretary's old brown Rolodex was still on the desk. He turned the knob on the Rolodex and the index cards spun round, fanning thirty years of partnerships and service.

The reception desk had been unoccupied long before Frank abandoned the office. The old photocopier, once the new robot, lay unplugged in the corner, dead and covered in a quarter-inch of dust. Inside the closet hung one of Frank's raincoats, with a tie slung over the shoulder.

He'd found Frank's office key in the study. He hadn't told anyone back home that he was going to the office. His phone buzzed in his coat pocket. It was Tara. 'Nowhere to park. Going to keep circling until I find something near.'

William opened the door to Frank's office, which looked as if it had been left in a hurry. Frank's drafting table stood by the window. On the ledge were some pens and the razor blades Frank used to scratch off the ink of his errors. The sticky patches left by old masking tape had gone black with dust. The black square angles on the white surface charted a chronology of all the blueprints Frank had worked on since he'd last cleaned the table with rubbing alcohol. William took a picture of the table with his phone, and pocketed the pens.

He closed the door behind him and went down the spiral staircase to the basement using his phone as a torch. In the basement was a door that led to the underground garage Frank had converted into his archive in the very early nineties. William tried the door. It was locked. He found the key on top of the ledge and unlocked it. The door opened a couple of inches, but stayed stuck. He threw his weight against the door and managed to shift some of the boxes that were blocking it from the inside.

He took out his phone and texted Tara. 'I forgot. My dad has a garage in the underground car park. Meet down there.'

The floor of the garage was covered in boxes and paper, and boxes of paper. William climbed over the mountain of paper to the garage door. It opened with no difficulty and the neons outside brightened the inside of the room. There were towering piles of boxes along the walls. Some had toppled long ago, spewing out their contents on top of other boxes. Some boxes had been eviscerated, perhaps to search for some vital document that had not reached its statute of limitations. He wondered how many trips it would take to get rid of all this shit. He picked up a tile catalogue advertising the new 1992 terrazzo collection.

Tara pulled up outside the garage with her car and opened the boot.

'Help me push the back seat down, will you?'

William walked over to the car to help.

'You're sure you wanna do this?'

William nodded.

'He's not going to be furious?'

He shrugged.

They started loading paper into Tara's car. William wasn't sure what it meant, to be here, with Tara, doing this – annihilating Frank's archive while Frank was in the hospital. He didn't know if this was helping. He didn't know for sure, but he thought it might be. He thought of his father, lost in the mountain at dusk. Lost in mountains of paper, with no electricity. Trying to find his way back home, back to the family, by the stars alone.

14. Epilogue
(or The World's Most Romantic Flashback)

LOIS HAD LEFT Joan alone with Frank at the hospital. This was one of those moments that could change the course of a history. Better to leave them to it. Tomorrow she would smuggle in something that Frank was not allowed to have. Maybe some salt.

Nick still hadn't called. She'd left a message earlier, about Frank. She wondered if he was out for New Year's Eve. The three of them had spent New Year's Eve at the hospital, drinking styrofoam cups of hot aspartame lemon from the vending machine. At one point Joan had sent William out for a bottle of wine. He'd come back with a bottle of cider, purchased from a crêpe restaurant behind the hospital. They toasted with polystyrene, to Frank's good health.

Lois brought her laptop to Frank's desk and opened it up. Her deadline for the war movie was in two days. The museum had sent a transcript of what needed translating. The title cards sounded like a history book. Like something the Historian might have written, if he'd been narrating the war in real time, and not in hindsight. They summarised key battles and introduced historical figures. Chronicled months of waiting in haunted, muddy trenches. Described the landscape of war, with its ghostly villages and towns, its pockmarked belfries and wildflower meadows that still bloomed under the bombs. Lois worked through them quickly, stopping and starting the film as she progressed with the titles.

Forty-seven minutes into the film, a woman walks onscreen pushing a wheelbarrow. A small child with blonde curls tags along beside her. The unwieldy wheelbarrow is piled high with sacks and a bucket of white laundry. The road is unpaved, which makes the task all the more difficult. Her husband is at war, which makes every task all the more difficult. He is at war, like the other husbands. But unlike the other husbands, he has given no news in a while.

She stops for a moment and leans against the wall of an old stone house. Her face pans up slowly, like a camera. She stares ahead, and the lens zooms in on her eye, until it is no longer recognisable as an eye but looks like a chalky puddle on a mountain, or the stomach of a ravine. Cut to a black screen with the word 'Vacherauville' flashing in white letters. Time, which is damage, has made the letters soft like a heartbeat. The name of the village flashes away, giving way to flashes of the villages. A square with chickens. A noticeboard. Barns that will one day be renovated and whose shutters will be painted royal blue. Like Brittany. Like the modernised barns Joan searches for online.

The woman looks beyond the dirt road, beyond the town, beyond her own child. She looks beyond, and sees the past.

And then: the world's most romantic flashback.

The village, poor and deserted, but at peace. Images of her husband fill the screen, one after another. Her husband smiling, being a man. Forking up hay. Bringing a glass of wine to his lips. Pulling on a pipe. Straddling a fence. Digging up the kitchen garden. All the things that make him happy.

The things that make one happy. A close-up of a blinking eye. A baby ignored for the memory of a man. Poor and deserted, but at peace. Before the insurrection, before the Jeep, before the J'Heap, before the man from Talahassee. The village like a heartbeat, pushing the fabric up and down, up and down.

Unlike the other husbands, Nick had given no news in a while.

To look back, you had to look beyond. Perhaps the opposite was true too. Perhaps to look beyond, you had to look past. A close-up of her blinking eye. The world's most romantic flashback. And having to go on, which is not the same as going beyond, and a kid tugging at your sleeve. Or no kid. But something tugging, because there was still a future to be experienced, with or without a husband. With or without a father. Without a baby or with one.

A close-up of a twitching eye. A close-up of a twitching heart.

The woman looks beyond the giraffe, beyond the edge of the bed and the shapes that lay there, back into the past. Beyond the white throw, which, together with the white sofa, looks like a lying woman covered in snow. With or without a husband. With or without a dog. With or without a father.

Everything doused in tears, real and not.

Meanwhile, a war is won. Depending on where you're standing.

The screen fades to black.

Acknowledgments

Thank you, Holly, Ursula and Ivy.

Thank you, Emily, Michael, Pamela and Patrice. Abel, Susan, Bill, Clare and Jamie. Marjorie and Ina.

Thank you, Emma Finn, Helen Francis, Jake Smith-Bosanquet, Alexander Cochran, Dorcas Rogers and Tracy England.